TEAM PARK

ANGELA AHN

TEAM PARK

tundra

Tundra Books, an imprint of Tundra Book Group,
a division of Penguin Random House of Canada Limited

Library and Archives Canada Cataloguing in Publication
Title: Team Park / Angela Ahn.
Names: Ahn, Angela, author.
Identifiers: Canadiana (print) 20230595642 | Canadiana (ebook) 20230595669 |
ISBN 9781774883433 (hardcover) | ISBN 9781774883440 (EPUB)
Subjects: LCGFT: Novels.
Classification: LCC PS8601.H6 T43 2024 | DDC jC813/.6—dc23

Published simultaneously in the United States of America by Tundra Books of Northern New York,
an imprint of Tundra Book Group, a division of Penguin Random House of Canada Limited

Library of Congress Control Number: 2023951966

Edited by Lynne Missen
Jacket designed by Gigi Lau
Typeset by Terra Page
The text was set in Minion Pro.

Printed in Canada

www.penguinrandomhouse.ca

1 2 3 4 5   28 27 26 25 24

Penguin
Random House
tundra | TUNDRA BOOKS

1

NOT SOCCER, OR RUGBY

"EVAN, ARE YOU SUPPOSED TO DO IT LIKE THAT?" Dad asked. Based on the way his hand was balled into a fist, I knew he wanted to take the weight out of my hand and do it himself.

I put my arms down by my side and tried to keep my back straight. We were standing in the living room at the front of the house where there was enough space for me to do my exercises.

"This is how Darren showed me." I blew the ends of my bangs out of my eyes.

He scrunched his nose. "Are you sure?"

Dad might know a lot about sports, but he wasn't there when I had my weekly physiotherapy appointments, was he?

"Positive."

"Okay. It's just that I want you to do it right."

"I know, I know."

Do it right was one of Dad's favorite sayings. But mostly what he meant was that I was doing it wrong.

"Maybe if this wrist heals up quick, you can rejoin the team." Dad looked at me carefully.

I tried to suppress my sigh. He really wanted me to "get back out there." I really wanted to never see my soccer cleats again. I did not miss standing in the muddy field on Sunday mornings and Wednesday nights. Nobody would miss me anyway. I only played when people couldn't make the matches. Instead, I had become the official water boy over the years.

"If only you had better balance, you never would have fallen off that skateboard," Dad said. The muscles in his neck tensed up.

It was a *longboard*. He should have known because he's the one who came home with it. He's the one who had said, "I heard at work that all the cool kids are riding these."

He now continued, "The round-robin playoffs started last week. Even though your team had a losing record, you could have still played. Maybe you still can. Finally pick up one of those nice little trophies they give out at the year-end banquet."

It was time to tell him. All these months away from it had made it pretty clear to me — I didn't miss soccer one tiny little bit. "Dad. I don't want to go back."

I watched Dad's eyes pop open wide. "What do you mean?"

"It's just that . . ." I struggled to come up with the right way to tell him.

"It wasn't Evan's thing," Lydia said loudly from the kitchen table. She was staring at her iPad. She snapped her gum before she added, "I mean, obviously."

Lydia, my older sister, had this way of speaking her mind easily. Just like that, the gum-popping teenager laid it all out there so simply. *It wasn't my thing.* I wished I knew what my *thing* was. Hockey hadn't worked out. I mean, all the *gear.* And I'd tried soccer for years, literally. The broken wrist had given me an excuse to stop. Now that I hadn't been playing these past few months, the thought of going back seemed about as appealing as eating Styrofoam peanuts.

Dad inhaled. "It's important for boys to do team sports."

Not this again. This was the battle Dad would fight to the end. The field he would die on. His personal preference would have been a rugby field as the combat zone, but at least he'd stopped trying to get me to do *that* sport after the summer camp a few years ago when the coach,

3

with two massive cauliflower ears, hinted that maybe I should try something else.

I looked hard at my dad. He was tall and stocky, with wide shoulders and a firm jaw that could have been used as an anvil. He was strong too — built like a tank. He stood out in a crowd. Not me. I must have missed out on the Park genes, because I just naturally looked like a zero you'd never notice. I might make a good spy one day, though. You wouldn't see me coming.

Part of me wanted to like soccer, or hockey, or rugby, and have Dad on the sidelines cheering for me. But wishing for it wasn't going to make it happen. I was going to be twelve at the end of the year, and if it hadn't happened by now, it wasn't going to. Team sports and Evan Park did not go well together.

"You learn a lot of life lessons," he continued when I failed to respond.

Like how to push people around over a ball?

"I don't do *team* sports," Lydia said. She lifted her eyes off the screen and leaned back in the chair to look at us.

"You're a girl, it's different."

Lydia almost fell to the ground.

"But you do a good job at gymnastics. Look at all your pretty ribbons!" He pointed to the glass IKEA display cabinet with five shelves. Dad's and Lydia's shelves were the fullest. Lydia had all her gymnastics medals and trophies, and Dad's shelf had something from every year he was on the high school rugby team. Even Mom had a typing award from the Stone Age, when they used typewriters. I'd seen one in a museum.

"*Pretty ribbons?*" Lydia repeated with outrage. "Rein in the stereotypes, Dad!" She huffed and crossed her arms.

At least Lydia had something good to put inside the cabinet. The only thing I had in there was a ribbon from a Sports Day two years ago. *Everybody* got a ribbon that day.

"Did I just hear something offensive?" Mom asked, as she emerged from the basement carrying a laundry basket on her hip. Mom shook her head and said quietly to Dad, "Honestly, John. You've got two girls. You can't think like that."

"I can't help the way I think," Dad huffed.

"Okay, then don't *talk* like that," Mom scolded. The corners of her eyes crinkled.

Dad sighed and turned to me. "Looks like the ladies don't want me to talk about guy stuff anymore."

I gave him the smallest of shrugs. *I* didn't want him to talk about "guy stuff" anymore either.

"Ev, just promise me you won't quit on team sports yet, okay?"

I said nothing because in my mind, I already had.

Georgia, my little sister and the only one with an emptier shelf in the cabinet than me, waddled into the living room. She wasn't wearing pants, only a very puffy pull-up diaper and a large, old hand-me-down T-shirt with a graphic of a Korean finger heart that a great-aunt from Busan had sent Lydia ages ago. It said something in Korean characters, but none of us could read Hangul — not even Mom or Dad. I hoped it didn't say anything embarrassing, because even *I* wore that tee when I was small.

She said in her squeaky toddler voice, "Yeah! Stop talking about sports!" Georgia pointed her spill-proof snack cup filled with Goldfish crackers at Dad and gave it a shake.

"I'd better just go somewhere and keep quiet," Dad grumbled. Putting his hand on Georgia's head as he walked by, he shuffled to the sofa in the family room at the back of the house and reached for the remote control. He said loudly, "Just keep doing your exercises, Ev. Make sure you do it right." Then he flicked on the TV, and I heard the opening music for SportsCentre.

He may as well have said, "Don't screw it up like you always do," because that's all I heard.

2

KIDS ONLY PHYSIO

DARREN STOOD ACROSS FROM ME IN THE THERAPY room. Once I started, he glanced down at his clipboard. It was challenging, but I finished the set of exercises where I had to bend a rigid bar of foam into a U-shape and then hold it like that for five seconds. I put the bar down on the table in the corner of the room. After ten reps, my hands and right wrist were weary, and I gave them a good shake.

Darren, wearing the same shorts and T-shirt he seemed to wear every week, had started doing squats while making notes. He was the most active twenty-something-year-old I had ever met. The guy just turned everything into an exercise. The muscles under the brown skin of his thigh bulged every time he bent his knees.

"Well, Evan, I have some bad news."

I felt my heart drop. "What is it?"

"I'm afraid you don't get to see my handsome face anymore." Darren held his hand out flat and rested his chin on it, like it was a mini stage, as he looked at me with a blank stare. His brown eyes were unreadable.

"What do you mean?" I asked.

"Your wrist! It's good! Normal range of motion, no discomfort. Every week you've been building up strength. There's really not much more I can do for you here. You've got your regular set of exercises — just keep them up." Darren pointed to things on the piece of paper on his clipboard. "With summer break coming up, it might be good for you to consider transitioning to some fun outdoor rehab activities anyway. Go to playgrounds, climb stuff, you know, that kind of thing."

I stared down at my wrist. Lately, it had felt a lot better. It wasn't exactly strong yet, but it was getting there.

"I am an excellent physiotherapist."

I smiled. "I thought this was only your part-time gig and that your real destiny was to climb to the top of Pinnacle Peak and press that button that unleashes a confetti bomb." I glanced at the souvenir posters Darren had hanging in the treatment room.

Darren had been to the last two regional auditions for the Dominator Ninja competition. He'd never quite made it to the semifinals, but still, he kept trying. I had to admire Darren's persistence. I imagine that it's not easy to keep failing at something, then dusting yourself off and going for it again.

I had seen a bunch of episodes on TV recently because Darren kept talking about how much fun he had while doing ninja training. Pressing that confetti bomb button once you successfully climbed a five-story tower looked like a pretty cool way to celebrate completing all the obstacles.

Darren laughed. "Well, sometimes a life's ambition doesn't pay the bills, unfortunately. But one day, I'm going to slam down that button and, *poof*, it's all going to rain down on me." He held out his arms, looked up to the sky, and acted like he was basking in the feeling of success.

It was easy to imagine Darren standing on the top of that tower, pumping his fist excitedly, screaming at the top of his lungs. The veins on the sides of his neck would have been bursting. "Have you ever wanted something badly, even though it didn't make much sense to other people?"

I shrugged. I wasn't sure I ever had, actually. "It does look pretty cool . . ." I admitted.

"So, you watched an episode?" Darren asked excitedly. He passed me a red squeeze ball.

"Well, yeah, because you kept talking about it, I wanted to see what the big deal was." I gripped the ball and held my fist tight before releasing. Darren didn't even need to bother with instructions at this point.

"It's so much fun and so satisfying at the same time. You should try it someday."

I laughed at the suggestion, even though *fun* and *satisfying* seemed like a pretty tough combination to beat. "Nah, I don't think it's for me. But I'm glad you like it."

Darren was the kind of guy that thought hiking up the trail called the Grouse Grind at seven on a Saturday morning was fun. Could I really trust the opinion of a person who climbed *up* the side of an entire mountain when there was a perfectly good gondola they could have taken instead?

"What? Ninja training can be for *anybody* and *everybody*. It's a whole bunch of different skills, stuff you'd never expect! But mostly, to me, it's like life, all represented on a ninja course. All the ups and downs. It's a giant metaphor for never quitting."

That sounded a lot like what Dad had said yesterday about *life lessons*. I looked at Darren, still unconvinced, and let him continue.

"Just when you think it's impossible and you want to give up, when you actually do manage to finish a hard obstacle, ah, man, it's an awesome feeling. The best part about ninja training, for me anyway, is that it's all about *me*, and what *I* can do."

"So, *not* a team sport," I muttered.

"Well, I have training *partners*, but yeah, not really a team thing." He tilted his head as he studied me. "Did you know, you've already got the ninja spirit?"

"Come on," I said in disbelief. "What are you talking about?"

"You, Evan Park, came to see me with a shriveled little right forearm and hand. When was that?" He checked his clipboard. "February twenty-seventh. Remember?"

How could I forget? When my cast had come off, not only did my skin smell disgusting, but it looked weird too. When I had put my two arms next to each other, they didn't even look like they belonged to the same person.

"You never quit. You did the work you needed to do. That's the ninja way." He held out his hand and I gave the ball one final squeeze before returning it.

Darren was starting to embarrass me now. All the stuff we had done at physio had been really hard and frustrating at first. But I did it. All of it. I kept doing it too.

Darren suddenly clasped his hands together. "I can see it. I can see you ninja training." He closed his eyes. "Oh! You are having so much fun!" He cracked open one eyelid. "C'mon. Close your eyes."

I reluctantly obeyed.

"Do you see yourself?"

I hadn't watched that many episodes of Dominator Ninja, but I had the gist of it. I stood across from Darren with my eyes closed, just like him. Then I tried to imagine it — me standing at the starting line. The crowd cheering and the bright lights illuminating the course.

I *could* see it. A wild thought came over me. Maybe *this* could be my thing. I shook my head and opened my eyes. It was silly.

"Come!" Darren ushered me out of the treatment room.

We walked into the waiting room, where Mom, Lydia, and Georgia were sitting.

Darren darted behind the reception desk and pulled out a small box. "Here." He handed it to me. "A parting gift."

Mom stood up and gathered the toys she had brought for Georgia to play with. "I'll guess we'll see you next week, Darren."

"No, you won't."

She stopped collecting toys. "What do you mean?"

"He's done! His wrist is all good. Not much more I can do for him now. Just continue doing the exercises you've been doing. But it's time to head outside and do things that are more fun than being in this office."

"Really?" she asked.

"Thank god," Lydia muttered. She blew a small bubble and then popped her gum. Her eyes were stuck firmly to her iPad.

"Ehbun strong?" Georgia asked. She was holding a doll and sitting on the floor. Her wispy hair had been done nicely with some bright hairclips when we got here, but they were in the doll's hair now.

Darren looked down at my little sister and said, "Evan really strong!" Darren flexed his bicep.

Nobody seemed to be able to talk to a three-and-a-half-year-old without sounding like a preschool teacher, not even Darren.

I held the box. "Should I open it?"

Darren nodded. I pulled the packing tape off and looked inside. There were several round lumpy objects, all brightly colored.

"What are these?" I asked.

"Hand holds. For climbing. You can mount them to a tree or the side of a building. You can start ninja training with these." Darren winked.

I stared into the box.

"Oh!" Darren clapped his hands together excitedly. "You know what! The next regional is in Seattle, last week of September — I'm going to drive down with a bunch of buddies to compete. And so could *you*! I think I saw something about a junior edition! You should look it up!"

"Junior edition?" I asked. Driving down to Seattle from Vancouver was an easy trip. I loved the exotic American fast-food stops — Jack in the Box, Ivar's, and Carl's Jr. Americans knew how to do deep-fried better than anybody. A trip to Seattle would be easy — and tasty.

"Junior what?" Georgia asked, pulling at my shorts.

"Dominator Ninja." I glanced down at her and tried to swat her away. "Never mind."

"What's *that*?" Georgia continued to hound me. Her round little face looked up at me, desperate for an answer.

"That's an opportunity for your big brother to do fun stuff over the summer to rehab his wrist," Darren said, leaning over to talk to Georgia.

Fun stuff. I *did* like the sound of that.

I glanced at Mom to gauge her reaction to what Darren was talking about, but she was in "Mom mode" — too busy packing up all of Georgia's things to really be paying attention.

"Now get outta here! But maybe I'll see you in Seattle in approximately fourteen weeks and four days?" Darren teased.

I shrugged, and before I even realized it, I laughed and said, "Sure. Maybe it will be my thing."

Lydia, now standing, gathered her long hair and brought it over one shoulder. She shot me a confused look, but I ignored it.

"Attaboy!" Darren patted my back.

Mom and my sisters said their goodbyes to Darren and waited for me in the doorway. I found myself lingering in the waiting room. I couldn't believe that I didn't have to come back to the Kids Only Physio office.

I turned to give Darren one final wave. Suddenly, I realized that I would miss Darren's confusing sense of humor and endless enthusiasm for ninja training.

Darren looked me straight in the eye. He held my gaze as he said, "Go ninja." And then, holding both his arms straight out, he did a deep squat.

3

SEATTLE IN THIRTEEN WEEKS?
IT DEPENDS...

I PULLED OUT THE ROLLED-UP POSTER FROM MY backpack.

"What's that?" Mom asked. It was a warm day, and she was wearing a plain black T-shirt. Her hair was pulled into a loose short ponytail.

I straightened out the paper and showed her. "It's my slogan for the summer."

She looked confused.

"It was my last school assignment." I shrugged. With this project, fourth grade was in the books.

"The Summer of Fun?" Mom asked, reading the poster.

I nodded.

The assignment Mr. Humberton gave us was to make a poster with a slogan for the summer. For him it might have been just a way to fill the time on the last day of the year, but for me, it also got me thinking about what I *really* wanted to do with the next nine weeks.

After my final session with Darren last week, I had watched a lot of YouTube videos of Junior Dominator Ninja events. The obstacles were similar to the adult competitions, just scaled differently. Events like jumping off platforms over a water pit, scaling rope ladders, and climbing walls by inserting pegs into strategically placed holes. Just a single kid versus a series of tough challenges. Their families all wore matching T-shirts and held up signs cheering them on.

The best part? There was no pushing and shoving other kids over balls.

After spending a lot of time watching all these videos, I started to think that learning how to be a ninja didn't seem like such a wild idea. Instead, it seemed like a summer plan.

"I like it!" Mom reached for a roll of tape before heading to the fridge. The problem with stainless steel is that magnets don't stick to it.

The fridge was like Mom's version of Dad's glass IKEA trophy cabinet. It felt pretty good watching her hang my poster. I couldn't remember the last time she had put anything of mine up.

Mom taped my poster next to a photograph of Lydia at her last gymnastics meet, where she'd won two medals, and Georgia's latest crayon scribble. For some reason, Mom was convinced Georgia had written down her initials: GP. The lines *sort of* looked like they *might* be a *G* and a *P*, but they were also just random lines. Depends on what you wanted to see, I guess.

I stood next to Mom as she carefully observed my drawing. Our shoulders were at the same height now. "I like how you drew little dots of rain over that tall evergreen tree in your picture. It's very Vancouver, isn't it?"

Any satisfaction I had felt seeing the poster up on the fridge was quashed. Art was often misinterpreted.

It wasn't *rain*, it was *confetti* coming down on me on top of the Space Needle in Seattle. I felt a little weird telling her that, so I just kept quiet.

"We don't have enough fun around here, do we?" Mom asked.

That was the truth.

"Totally," Lydia agreed from her seat at the kitchen table. I hadn't even noticed her. While just sitting there, she was managing to do three things at once: watching a YouTube video on her iPad; shoving a Danish in her mouth; and balancing on just the rear legs of her chair. She was wearing one of her extra-enormous, mega-oversized hoodies. One day, Lydia was going to disappear inside one of those hoodies and we'd never find her.

"The timing of this poster is so good." Mom smiled mysteriously before looking at her watch.

"What do you mean?" I asked.

"It's going to arrive at any time."

"What is it?" I hoped Mom hadn't done too much online shopping. Dad had what I will call a "moment" when he saw how many empty Amazon boxes there had been in last week's recycling.

"You'll see." Mom smiled.

As if on cue, the doorbell rang. Mom dashed to the front door, and I followed behind.

"I hope that's not another order from the suffocating online monopoly," Lydia said, finally taking her eyes off her screen.

We glanced at each other. Lydia had seen how Dad had reacted to the boxes in the recycling too.

"Well, it's *not* from Amazon," Mom said over her shoulder. "I shopped local this time."

I looked out the front door as Mom opened it. There was a delivery truck parked in front of our house. Written across the side of it: *Jumping for Joy.*

"Jumping for Joy?" I asked.

Lydia's kitchen chair clattered to the ground, but she was on her feet. "The *TRAMPOLINE* company?" Lydia shrieked.

"Surprise!" Mom beamed. She turned to the delivery person. "Please bring it around to the backyard."

A surprise backyard trampoline? The Summer of Fun was officially *on.*

"Why is there a truck blocking the garage?" Dad asked from the front door. The four of us were standing at the back of the house, watching the two men set up the trampoline.

We all turned around to look at him.

"You're early!" Mom quickly walked up to him.

"Ah, nothing but headaches today," Dad grumbled. "The city shut down the site because of some minor code violation. It's embarrassing. My boss is not going to be impressed."

Dad's new job was as the project manager for a big condo tower going up in the Guildford neighborhood. It was his biggest project to date.

"What are you all looking at?" he asked. He hung up his windbreaker on the hook by the back door.

"I bought the kids something." Mom added quickly, "So they can have fun this summer."

Dad peered out the window with us.

"A trampoline?" he exploded.

His voice had such an angry edge, I was startled. Georgia had just come down from her nap, and she jumped too before grabbing on to Mom's leg.

"It was on sale," Mom said defensively. She placed her hand on Georgia's shoulder.

Dad looked unimpressed and took measured breaths. "Grace, you did not have my permission to buy this. All those boxes last week!" He gritted his teeth before he continued, "You should have consulted me at least! Those things are like childhood injuries waiting to happen." He pointed his finger at the backyard.

"Says the man who thinks tackling other men is perfectly normal behavior." Mom crossed her arms in front of her chest. "They're just about finished with setup. It's done."

Dad blew very hot, very angry air through his nose. "Let's discuss this *later*."

Lydia and I glanced at each other.

Dad headed to the refrigerator. He gazed briefly at my Summer of Fun poster before opening the door and retrieving a beer.

He snapped it open and took a big guzzle before heading to the sofa. I held my breath waiting for Dad to say something about the poster, but he never did.

After the trampoline crew left, my sisters and I made a beeline for it. Mom came outside with a cup of barley tea and watched us, while Dad stayed inside. Dad had made it pretty clear how he felt about it, but why could he not see how *amazing* it was to have a trampoline in the backyard? His crabby mood would not stop us from enjoying it. Like Mom had said: *It was done*. May as well have some fun with it.

The trampoline was a wide oval with mesh netting all around it — a literal industrial-strength zippered safety net to keep jumpers inside. How could this be dangerous? Sometimes Dad was just plain ridiculous!

It was placed in the perfect spot, on the patch of grass where Dad had previously set up a small net for us to kick balls into. Goodbye soccer net, hello trampoline!

The first steps onto its surface made my knees feel a bit wonky. But once I got used to it, I bounced, and I bounced some more. Lydia was already really good at jumping and doing twists and turns in the air from all those years at gymnastics class.

"Fun, right?" Mom said from the deck.

I gave her a thumbs-up and, despite spending a lot of time falling on her butt, Georgia giggled happily, "Bouncy, bouncy!"

The timing of everything was so perfect. First, no more school, and now we had *this* to keep us busy. All my friends were gone all summer anyway. Aaron had a big extended reunion at his family's cottage, and Davey had already left to spend his summer with his grandmother in China. Who needed friends when we had a new bouncy trampoline? But I'd send them a picture of it later for sure.

Flying through the air made me feel so *free*. No rules, no ref blowing a whistle at me. It was just me (I was pretending that my sisters weren't there) and the gravity-defying spring of a new trampoline.

As I leapt, I thought about some of the Junior Dominator Ninja events I had watched recently — many of them involved trampolines. Sometimes competitors had to run and use a trampoline as a springboard to a net or a wall or a bar. I was ninja training *already* and I didn't even realize it until just this moment! I thought Darren would approve. No wrists or hand strength involved, but still, I needed to get good at bouncing to do a ninja course. This was a good start.

If I was going to get serious about ninja training, I'd better come up with a list of supplies. Even if Dad didn't like it, I thought Mom would be okay buying me stuff, just so long as it was all toward the goal of me getting my wrist back to its old self. Not to mention the added benefit of physical activity and fresh air!

I started wondering about how else we could transform the backyard into my own personal ninja course. I stopped jumping and moved to the edge of the trampoline to start visualizing.

There were a few big trees that separated our yard from the neighbor's. That was the perfect place for the climbing holds Darren had given me. The trunks were wide and sturdy. But I was going to need a few more things. I started listing things off in my head:

☐ Salmon ladder
☐ Water pit
☐ Hanging rings
☐ Warped wall
☐ Balancing stuff – Crates? Boxes?

All that stuff wasn't too expensive, was it?

"What are you thinking about, Ev? Everything okay?" Mom asked.

"Do you think we can hang the climbing holds now? We keep putting it off."

Lydia and Georgia were still bouncing, and my knees buckled to keep my balance.

"Sure, there's a bit of time before I have to start dinner. It shouldn't take too long." She put down her cup and headed for the garage.

I unzipped the netting and started to crawl out.

"Are you done already?" Lydia asked. She did a backflip.

"No, I'll be back."

"When you get back, you can double-jump me."

Mom emerged from the garage with a ladder, a hammer, and the box of climbing holds.

"Do you think we should ask Dad for help?" I asked. "Where is he anyway?"

She shrugged. "I can do it." Her eyes had a determined look.

We set up the ladder at the base of the tree we picked while Lydia and Georgia continued to play.

"What are you two doing?" Dad asked loudly. He was standing on the deck with his hands on his hips.

I wasn't sure how long he'd been watching us.

"We're just hanging stuff," Mom replied without looking at him.

"Why didn't you ask me? That's not a job for either of you." He strode down the stairs and quickly crossed the lawn.

Mom ignored him. "I'm perfectly capable of using a hammer."

"Just give it to me." He practically yanked it from her hand.

I saw her mouth pucker. "Fine, do it yourself. Evan, I'm going inside." She turned quickly to leave.

"Now, tell me what this is all about. What are you planning on hammering into this tree?"

I held the box awkwardly in my hands. It would have been better to do this with Mom. I cleared my throat before I answered. "Darren, you know, the physio, gave me these. They're climbing hand holds."

Dad looked inside. "Oh."

"He said they would be good for strength training."

At first Dad didn't say anything. He just looked at the box and then me. Finally, he said, nodding, "Not a bad idea at all for you to be out here keeping busy. You definitely need to get stronger."

I swallowed hard. I mean, Dad was right, but still, the way he said it, it stung a tiny bit.

"We were going to use this tree here." I patted the trunk.

Dad shook his head. "No, that's not a good idea. See how it leans? You want a straighter tree."

I knew from watching videos of people scaling walls in ninja competitions that sometimes an angled surface was actually a good thing, but I just let Dad decide. That way he could do it right.

After dinner, the three of us headed out to the trampoline again. How could we not? But I had eaten too much, and my guts felt a bit queasy after just a few jumps. I needed a drink of water, so I headed back inside the house.

As soon as I stepped inside, I heard my parents. They were upstairs arguing. I didn't *want* to eavesdrop, but I couldn't help it. Their voices were really loud. I bet if Lydia and Georgia hadn't been so noisy outside on the trampoline, we could have heard them from the backyard too.

"It's *such* a bad idea!" Dad said loudly.

"I don't understand why you're so against it! Lydia is going to love it. She already loves it!"

"It's not Lydia I'm worried about! It's Evan! That boy is such a klutz. He's probably going to break something else!"

I felt my face flush.

"But you know what? That's not even the main point. The main point is all your small little purchases are bad enough — you had no right to make this big purchase without asking me!" Dad said. "*I'm* the breadwinner here! You should have asked me!"

I held my breath.

"Did you just say *breadwinner*? Gah! I don't need your permission to buy things!" Mom yelled.

"You're just throwing money around, but you never make any."

"*Excuse me?*"

I threw my hands up to cover my ears. I had heard enough, and I had heard it all before — today, it was just a different version.

Without even getting a glass of water, I went back outside.

I sat on the stairs and tried to calm down. I wanted to forget about what I had just heard — pretend like I hadn't heard anything. Instead, I focused on watching Lydia. Lydia could do almost anything she wanted with her body. Flips, twists, you name it, she could do it. It was impressive, but somehow annoying at the same time. I couldn't do what she could. Not even close. Watching Lydia wasn't helping at all.

I huffed. Dad's words still echoed around my head. *Breadwinner*. Who even talks like that? But that wasn't even the word I couldn't shake.

Klutz.

Was that what Dad really thought of me? I clenched my jaw while I stared at my wrist. The fall off the longboard had been an *accident*. It's like he thought I had run over that cracked concrete on *purpose*.

My whole life everything had been chosen for me. Forced on me, even. It was always stuff Dad had wanted me to do — including that annoying longboard. I hated all of it. It wasn't me. It was what *he* wanted me to be.

For the first time, what *I* wanted was something for myself. Darren said I could do it. Darren said I was already doing it; I just hadn't realized.

I felt more determined than ever to find my own way. Find my own thing. Finally, I knew what it was. Go ninja!

4

MY THING

I WAS HANGING ON WITH EVERYTHING I HAD. I gripped the climbing holds with the tips of my fingers and counted. I wasn't even using my feet at all. *One, two, three, four, FIVE.* I dropped to the ground and gulped air. FIVE! Just yesterday, the first time I had tried the holds, I could only count to three. *This* was progress.

"Yes!" I yelled.

I did a very energetic fist pump that resulted in me almost falling down. As I stumbled to regain my balance, I looked around to see if anybody had been watching.

Then our eyes met. Mom was standing by the open kitchen window. I felt a twinge of self-consciousness.

She smiled before sticking her face out the window.

"Don't worry about it. Remember? What's your slogan for the summer?"

I appreciated the reminder. "The Summer of Fun!"

"So, have fun!" she yelled back. She went back to whatever magic she performed to make us yummy dinners.

"Are you doing physio exercises?" Lydia snapped her gum. "You've been out here all afternoon." I startled because I hadn't even seen her come outside.

I contemplated whether or not to tell her.

"Hello? Earth to Evan!" Lydia said when I didn't answer her.

"Promise me you won't make fun?" I leaned against the tree.

"Come on. I don't make fun. I tease. Lovingly." She blinked in an exaggerated way.

I let out a small laugh. "Don't mock me, okay?"

She nodded.

Nothing sarcastic came out of her mouth, so I decided to trust her. "It's sort of physio related. But I'm actually ninja training."

She scrunched up her entire face. "Like Darren suggested?"

"Yeah, I guess."

"Oh." She looked away. "It's really hard not to make fun of you right now."

I tilted my head and glared at her.

"Okay, first of all, you have to realize that use of the word 'ninja' is total cultural appropriation, right?"

"Huh?"

"Like, historically, ninja were highly trained Japanese assassins or something, right?"

"I guess so."

"Is it okay to use the word 'ninja' to describe a person who does an obstacle course?" Lydia raised her eyebrows.

"I don't know, so I guess you'll tell me . . ." Sometimes Lydia took her job as the eldest and most culturally and socially aware sibling seriously.

"I guess it's supposed to be a kind of *compliment* or something, but I don't think we should take from other people's cultures without realizing it. It's totally insensitive."

I'd never looked at a word like *ninja* in that way before. "But *I'm* not taking anything!"

"Not *you*, but the Dominator Ninja people already took it. Just be aware of what it is, okay?"

"Okay, I acknowledge cultural app . . . Wait, what is it again?" I asked.

"Appropriation."

"Cultural appropriation."

"Good. Like, if I ever catch you wearing a tacky ninja costume or anything grotesquely outrageous like that, you're going to get an earful, got it?"

"I wouldn't dare." She'd already given me and my parents the inappropriate-Halloween-costume-talk ages ago.

"Now that we've cleared that up, tell me why you want to be a 'ninja.'" She quoted with her fingers. "Oh, I hate saying the word in this context." Her whole body convulsed as if she had swallowed something nasty.

"I'm trying to . . . get better. Darren said that ninja training could be for anybody. Plus, I have to rehab my wrist anyway, don't I? Can't I have fun and rehab at the same time?"

Lydia raised her eyebrows.

"The Dominator Ninja: Junior Edition competition in Seattle is on September twenty-eighth."

She bit her bottom lip and averted her eyes.

"What?" I asked, slightly annoyed.

"I just have to ask. Why all this, all of a sudden?"

The answer was simple but complicated.

"Because . . . you have gymnastics and gum-popping. I . . . I don't have anything. Yet."

"Ah," Lydia said, nodding. "Your *thing*."

"Yeah, I'm not sure ninja stuff is my thing, but I know soccer sure isn't. Or hockey. And especially not rugby!" My shoulders sagged a little. "I just want to find something for *me*. Maybe I'll even be good at it. For once." My empty shelf in the glass cabinet was never going to get filled by doing what Dad wanted. But what if I filled it by doing something *I* wanted? "Go bounce on the trampoline or something. Leave me alone and let me practice." I knew I had a long way to go and almost getting ridiculed by my sister was eating into training time.

"Okay, I gotta respect the attitude. And I'll leave you alone, but only if you double-jump me," Lydia said.

I sighed.

Dad had made a call last night to one of his usual guys. He had a huge contact list on his phone of people who did different things for his job sites. The guy who owned a local print shop was a friend of his from high school — a buddy from the rugby team.

Overnight, we suddenly had a sign. It was printed on a sturdy, waterproof plastic sheet with holes punched in the corners. Dad attached it to the zippered entrance of the trampoline using zip ties.

PARK FAMILY TRAMPOLINE RULES:

1. Three people maximum.
2. Sweep the surface clean before using (dry broom, not wet broom).
3. **ALWAYS, ALWAYS** enclose yourself with the zipper before jumping.
4. Give other jumpers lots of space.
5. No double-jumping.

"You know we're not supposed to," I reminded Lydia as I pointed to the sign.

"He's not here." Lydia started to climb onto the trampoline. "Hurry up." She glanced over her shoulder, completely ignoring Dad's rules.

"You know it's a clear violation of Rule Number 5."

"Oh, it's fine. He's too strict. I get double-jumped at Jen's house *all the time*. I've been double-jumped at gymnastics class by the *teachers*! And they wouldn't do it if it wasn't safe," she said with a silly grin on her face. "I'll start jumping and then, you join in. I'll go flying. But you've got to time it just right."

I dusted off my hands before I climbed through the netting. Then I zipped us up inside.

"I do this, and you leave me alone, right?"

She was only fourteen years old, but Lydia was cagey. Somehow, she always knew how to get what she wanted.

"I don't say things lightly. My word is my word." Despite sounding serious, Lydia looked ridiculously happy right now.

How could one person love double-jumping so much? People were always surprised when they found out we were siblings — they said we looked nothing alike. It was true. Lydia had a narrow face and a pointy chin; I had a square jaw and high cheekbones. Her hair was fine and wispy, mine was rough and thick. Genetics are unpredictable, I guess.

I was just about to bend my knees and send her into the air when Mom called.

"Evan!" Mom stood on the back porch.

"What?"

Lydia and I both stopped bouncing.

"Georgia's asking for you!"

I did a face palm.

"*Please?*" Mom begged. "She only napped for about fifteen minutes."

A mere fifteen-minute nap was almost worse than no nap. Georgia was probably driving her bonkers.

I didn't move. Mom knew how I felt about Georgia asking for me like this.

Lydia sighed loudly. "Will I never get doubled-jumped on this thing?" She sat down roughly. "Just go already."

"But it's literally the worst job," I complained.

"Now you're just being dramatic. There are plenty of worse jobs." Lydia rolled her eyes.

"You're just lucky Georgia doesn't ask for *you*," I snorted.

"Evan?" Mom pleaded. She clasped her hands together. "I saw that you're really enjoying those climbing holds Darren gave you. Do you need something else? I can order things for you!"

She had moved more swiftly than usual to the bribes-for-good-deeds phase of begging.

"Well, I was thinking I could use a few more things . . . For rehab!"

"Seriously?" Lydia sounded disgusted, and her jaw dropped.

From the open window upstairs, I heard Georgia yell, "I want Ehbun!"

"Whatever you need. Just come inside, please," Mom said.

"Have you no shame?" Lydia said through clenched teeth. "Don't ask her to buy you stuff! We just got this." She pointed down to the trampoline.

I whispered back, "I'm not *asking*, she's *offering*."

"His moral compass is broken!" Lydia threw her hood over her head and flung herself down on the trampoline. "I guess there's no double-jumping for me right now, either!"

"It's not like it's a frivolous demand. It's for *rehab*."

Lydia muttered, "Sure, justify your greed as best as you can."

A big brother forced into an unpleasant job needs to be compensated *somehow*. Fair is fair.

5

THE GREAT ESCAPE

"UPSTAIRS?" I ASKED. AS IF GEORGIA WOULD BE anywhere else.

Mom nodded. She looked tired.

The upstairs washroom was the only one with enough space for me to sit next to Georgia and read to her while she sat on the toilet. At three-and-a-half, Georgia was not "toilet independent."

That's the nice way to say that Georgia still needed pull-up diapers because of the occasional "accident."

"Thank you!" Mom added.

"So, can I show you some of the stuff I would like to order later? For my rehab?"

"Sure." Mom dumped a container of marinated bulgogi into a large skillet.

"A plastic liner may be involved. Don't be concerned."

"A plastic liner?" The meat sizzled and she pushed it around with a wooden spoon.

"For the water pit."

"Ehbun!" Georgia yelled.

"Did you just say *water pit*?" Mom asked.

"Yup! Gotta go, Georgia needs me!" I raced upstairs.

"Ehbun, is that you?" Georgia's squeaky voice echoed in the bathroom.

"Yes, it's me."

"You took too long." She was sitting on the throne, waving a book in the air. "This one! This one!"

I leaned against the doorframe. "When will you be able to read this to yourself?"

"I'm *three*," Georgia replied. "And a half!" She practically threw the book at me. "Maybe next month."

She was actually closer to four, but I did *not* want to argue with her about it.

I stepped into the washroom and looked at the book on the ground. Oh no. Not this one again. Just the look of the cover made me feel dead inside. It was a book about a hedgehog who befriended a unicorn. The hedgehog had rainbow quills. The unicorn wore Birkenstocks. The book never explained why.

And it *rhymed*. After repeatedly reading it, I had the darn thing *memorized*. Not out of choice, but because it had cruelly wormed its way into my memory. I had asked myself maybe a hundred times why Georgia needed me to read to her while she tried to do her business, but not once had there been a satisfactory or reasonable answer.

"Best funny book." Georgia giggled at the mere thought of the story.

Then, suddenly, she stood up. She kicked off her pull-up and started to run. "Need second-best book!"

I made a grab for my escaping sister, but the little rascal dodged me. I wasn't sure how a toddler had moves like that, but she dipped her shoulder and *escaped* — the move was NFL-worthy.

"Get back here!"

She was already in the hallway, but I pounced and grabbed her shoulder.

"Gotcha!" I surprised myself with my speed. I had put a quick end to the Great Bathroom Escape. Those warm-up lunges I'd practiced with Darren had come in handy after all!

As I reeled her in, Georgia laughed hysterically. Then she said, "Whoops." We both stared down at the wet carpet.

After a bit of heated back and forth, Dad went to the grocery store to rent a carpet cleaner. Mom thought it could wait, but Dad didn't agree.

Dad lugged it upstairs by himself while Mom stood by the washroom with her arms crossed.

"It's so late! Why can't we just do it tomorrow?" She sighed irritably.

"Maybe you think it's fine leaving pee soaking into the carpet, but I think that's disgusting."

I lingered in the hallway, in front of my room.

Dad filled the machine with detergent and plugged it in.

"Remember, Georgia, you are not a dog. We go in the toilet." Dad poked his finger against her chubby little cheek.

I half expected Dad to get angry at her, but he never did. For some reason, I wasn't relieved. I was *bothered*.

"But Ehbun was too funny!" Georgia imitated the way I had lunged at her. She was, like everybody else, in her pajamas, waiting to go to bed.

"Don't blame *me*, you little escape artist! You could have just asked me to get the book you wanted."

"Ehbun don't know how to find second-best book. It's in a secret spot," Georgia whispered.

I stared at her, confused. What *was* this second-best book anyway?

Dad finally started up the machine. What a racket.

"Well, this sucks," Lydia said over the noise. She stood in the hallway with a scowl on her face. She popped her gum out of her mouth and flicked it into the garbage can.

"I'll be done soon! Don't forget to brush your teeth!" Dad yelled in Lydia's direction.

"The package says, 'Prevents Cavities'!" Lydia turned and closed her door.

Mom had disappeared downstairs. That was a pretty smart move. It wasn't fun being up here right now.

Dad pushed the carpet cleaner back and forth, keeping his eyes straight down to see what he was doing, but eventually he glanced up at me and said loudly, "You should have been more responsible and not allowed this to happen."

Without answering him, I went into my room and closed the door. I plunked myself down on my bed and stared up at the ceiling. It was hard for me to imagine how I could have controlled Georgia's bladder, but somehow, in Dad's eyes, I had managed to screw up again.

6

STUMPED

I STOOD IN THE BACKYARD HOLDING THE IPAD AT arm's length and snapped a selfie with the trampoline in the background.

I contemplated what message I should send Aaron and Davey with the photo. All I could come up with was: Bet you wish you were here! I pressed the arrow to send it.

Then I typed: Making my own ninja course!

But I realized that *one* obstacle and *one* trampoline wasn't exactly a proper course, and it wasn't really brag worthy. I deleted the second message. I'd send another message when there was more stuff, cooler stuff, to show them.

There was no doubt about it — the yard needed more work. I headed to the garage hoping to find something to supplement my ninja training. Having fun required a lot of equipment.

I hadn't nudged Mom about the stuff she had promised to get for me, because given how Dad reacted to the trampoline and his frustration about the carpet-cleaning incident, I wasn't sure he was going to be too happy about Mom spending *more* money. I was going to find the right time to remind her soon, but now wasn't it. While I waited, I needed more stuff *now*. Free stuff.

The garage was full of odds and ends Dad didn't want to throw away because they *might* come in handy one day. There was bound to be something good in here.

I had my head stuck in a box when Dad barged in.

"Ev? What are you doing?"

I practically jumped. "Oh geez, you scared me." I steadied myself. "I'm just looking for stuff."

"Like what?"

I examined my father. It was a warm July Saturday morning — it was hard to believe that school had been out for a week already! Dad was dressed casually in an old T-shirt, shorts, and sandals. Dad's sturdy frame was always imposing. He hadn't shaved, and stubble poked out around his square jaw.

"For . . . my wrist rehab. Darren said I should keep busy." I was deciding whether or not to mention ninja training to Dad. Something about how he had blamed me for the pee on the carpet last night and the way he looked this morning — his jaw tight, his eyes piercing — made me hesitate.

"What's wrong with the weights and stuff you were doing before?"

"Nothing. I can still do that. But I just want to do something that's a bit more . . . fun, you know?" I quickly added, "Also challenging."

"Oh, I see." Dad walked to the back of his truck and opened the tailgate. I saw that it was full of tree stumps.

I was suddenly reminded of an obstacle from Dominator Ninja I had seen on YouTube last night when I was trying to ignore all the fuss Dad was making with the carpet cleaner.

"What are those stumps for?" I asked.

Dad had climbed up to move them out of his truck.

"Firewood or something. We had to cut down a couple of trees on-site yesterday. Thought they might come in handy, so I brought them home."

"Can I have them?" I asked. I walked up to the truck to have a closer look. They were irregular in size. They were perfect. I imagined spacing them out across the backyard and leaping from one to the next. It was a balance test.

"What do you want stumps for? How are these useful for wrist rehab?" Dad pulled the first stump down to the garage floor.

"Well," I started before I faltered. Why was it so hard to talk to him? I wished I were more like Lydia in moments like this.

"Well, what?"

"I thought, maybe, I'd do some . . . ninja training." As I spoke, my heart started to pound fiercely.

"Ninja training?"

"Have you ever seen that show on TV? Dominator Ninja?"

I watched his face for any signs of recognition.

His eyes narrowed. "*You* want to do *that*? Hanging off poles like a monkey is more up Lydia's alley, isn't it? It doesn't seem like a *real* sport."

My cheeks flared up. "I know it's not rugby." I swallowed hard. "But I'm trying to . . ." I lost my energy. I couldn't say it out loud. I wanted to say, *I'm trying to find my thing.* Instead, I told Dad, "It's for balancing."

Dad stopped moving stumps. "Yeah, you could improve there, for sure." Then he shrugged indifferently. "Sure, take the stumps."

I bit my lip and took a deep breath. Finding the logs to turn into an obstacle should have made me feel happy, but instead, my chest tightened. I tried to lift one, but I couldn't. Dad nudged me aside and dropped the stump I couldn't lift onto the cement floor of the garage. The only way I could help to move it was to roll it out of the garage.

Behind me, carrying a stump with both arms, Dad started curling it like a giant dumbbell. "Hey, here's a good use for them! They *are* handy!" He laughed.

I forced myself to smile.

I kept rolling my stump until I was a few feet away from where Dad had dropped his. I positioned it so that a cut end stayed steady against the grass. When we were done moving all the pieces from the truck onto the grass, I placed everything in a way that was similar to the obstacle I had seen last night. Not in a straight line, but in a slight zigzag pattern. Dad watched and after a while said, "Shouldn't they be farther apart?"

I stepped back. I knew what was going to happen.

Dad started to rearrange everything the way he liked. When he was done, he said, "Okay. That looks good. Give it a go."

Reluctantly, I stepped onto the closest stump. I glanced over at Dad. I wished he wasn't here. I wished I could practice alone. This was supposed to be *my* thing, and I really didn't want an audience with *opinions*. But he didn't look like he was going anywhere. The next stump was farther than I would have placed it. But I tried it anyway. Leaping with my right leg extended, I knew I wasn't going to make it. I landed on the grass instead.

Dad shook his head. "No, Ev. That's not how you do it. Let me show you." He stood on the log I had just been on. "I used to be a pretty good athlete, you know."

I tried very hard not to openly sigh.

"We know, Dad, you *tell* us all the time," Lydia said from the trampoline. "Why don't you *show* us?"

Both Dad and I startled at the sound of her voice.

Lydia blew a large, pink bubble.

Dad glared at her briefly before resuming the task at hand. He hunched over and stared intensely at the logs in front of him. He slapped his thighs and rubbed them down. Then he jumped. He couldn't make it to the next one either.

I raised my eyebrows but stayed silent.

"Huh. I guess they're a bit too far," Dad admitted. One by one, he started to shift everything. "If it's too hard for me, you definitely won't be able to do it."

It looked like Dad was in one of those moods when it was best to give him space and time. I joined Lydia on the trampoline.

We watched Dad silently. It took several attempts for him to find the right spacing. After he managed to easily jump the whole line of stumps without falling off, Dad stood at the end of the line and nodded with satisfaction.

Mom yelled out the open kitchen window, "Lunch!"

"Oh, great, I'm starving!" Dad abandoned the stumps and hustled to the house. "Ev, those are ready for you now. You should be able to do it with a lot of practice."

"We'll just be a minute!" Lydia called back. I got up to go inside too, but Lydia grabbed my hand. "Wait!"

"Why?" I asked.

"You okay?"

I shrugged. "Why wouldn't I be?"

"Okay . . . I was just asking."

I headed inside with my jaw tight. Dad was right about one thing. I was going to practice. Then he'd see.

7

ADVENTURE AWAITS

DARREN HAD TOLD ME I SHOULD GO TO A playground and climb stuff. Cheap and easy. I hadn't been to a playground in ages, but today, since the weather was bright and not too hot for the second week of July, I decided it was a good day to diversify my training schedule.

I filled up my water bottle and slipped into my running shoes. Georgia looked up from her spot in the living room and said, "Ehbun go to trampoline?"

"Nah, I'm going to the park."

"Want to go with your *sisters*?" Mom asked from the kitchen.

The answer was a resounding *no*. "Well, I kind of wanted to go by myself . . ." I admitted.

Georgia raced to grab my leg. "Take Georgia! Take Georgia!"

Lydia sprinted down the stairs and, copying Georgia, said, "Take Lydyah! Take Lydyah!" She squatted down to the ground and grabbed my other leg.

The two of them started to giggle. I felt like a eucalyptus tree with too many unwanted koala bears attached to me.

I sighed. "Fine, come with me. But I'm going to Rideau Adventure Playground, not the closer one. You have to be willing to walk farther, okay, Georgia?"

"Georgia can do!" She let go and grabbed her shoes off the shoe rack.

Lydia followed her. "Seriously, I've got nothing going on this morning. My gymnastics practice is in the afternoon. I'm coming too."

"Just don't get in my way, okay?" I begged.

"Don't get in *my* way!" Georgia threatened.

Rideau Adventure Playground was always busy because it was the biggest and best park in the neighborhood. As expected, there were a bunch of other kids around, but it was not as busy as it would get later in the day.

It was full of unique structures that no other playground had: crisscrossed giant logs, a huge twisty slide that was two stories high, and all the poles and ropes you could possibly imagine.

It hadn't changed, but *I* had. Before, I used to just see it as a place to *play*, but now, it was a place to *train*. This playground equipment was basically a free ninja course.

When we got closer, my eyes zoomed in on the rock wall with colorful hand holds in all sorts of different shapes and sizes. It was much more complex and challenging than the holds we had nailed up on the backyard tree.

"We have to take turns watching Georgia," Lydia reminded me as I was just about to sprint for the rock wall.

"Oh, right." This is why I had wanted to come *alone*.

"Go ahead," Lydia said. "You go do what you want first."

"Thanks. Call me when you want a break."

We split up and I ran to the rock wall. I stood in front of it and craned my neck slightly to look up to the top. It seemed about ten feet high — slightly taller than the height of the ceiling in my bedroom. A good challenge, but not *too* high.

In an effort to hype myself up, I slapped my hands together twice before I whacked my thighs. I'd seen a lot of the participants on Dominator Ninja do the same thing on TV, and Dad had done it before he tried jumping the stumps. It was something athletes did.

I puffed out a few nervous breaths before I reached for the hand holds.

Straightening my arm, I put my right hand up and reached for the red knob comfortably within reach. My left hand gripped a blue hand hold at about shoulder level. I stepped up onto a green hold, just above the ground, with my right foot and swiveled my toe against the hold to make sure it was secure.

Then, I climbed.

My left foot found a hold, and then my right hand let go and reached for another one, about fifteen centimeters higher. Carefully, I moved only one limb at a time. Before I knew it, I was on top of the wall, straddling it.

"Yes! I did it!" I shouted to my sisters.

Georgia was climbing up a rope ladder to reach the top of a high, wobbly walking bridge. She looked back at me and said flatly, "That's nice," and resumed climbing. She was pretty fast at it. Surprisingly fast.

Lydia glanced up, raised her shoulders slightly, and gave me a thumbs-up. But it felt like a thoroughly sarcastic thumbs-up. She went back to standing behind Georgia with her hands behind Georgia's back, ready just in case she tumbled backward. But Georgia never fell. She reached the top of the ladder quickly and yelled, "See, I did it too!"

Humph. Obviously, they had no idea what a big deal this was!

As swiftly as I climbed up, I scrambled back down the other side of the wall and then headed toward the main play structure. There was a long line of monkey bars, but not the boring classic straight row. These bars were set up as an S-curve. That was my next challenge. All arms, no feet helping me at all.

I grabbed the first bar and adjusted my grip. I wasn't sure how long I'd be able to hold on.

Before my strength gave way, I reached for the next bar. And then the next. I did six rows before I had to drop to the ground. I looked at my hands in disbelief. They were stronger than I could have hoped for!

"Hey, that wasn't bad!" Lydia said. She had been watching me as she sat on top of a high platform with her legs dangling down. "That's tough to do when you're not used to it."

"Ehbun strong!" Georgia said. She stood in the middle of a shaky bridge, jumping on it so the whole thing rattled.

I smiled. And I was just getting started.

8

THE BASICS

MOM GOT THE BANDAGES READY. THE ONE blister on my hand that had popped seriously hurt. The other two were on the verge of ripping open too. I winced even though she barely brushed the skin.

"If you keep doing it, you'll get calluses like me." Lydia showed me her palms. At the base of each finger was a little patch of dull, hard skin.

Soft skin was a setback I hadn't anticipated. But the morning at Rideau Adventure Playground had proven I was definitely regaining my strength.

"You should take it easy," Mom said. She rubbed some antibiotic ointment onto the bandage.

"I can't. I don't have much time." Training was important. I had to keep at it.

"Time for what?"

"Dominator Ninja," Lydia said in an ominous, deep, and booming voice. She threw her hood over her head at the same time, just to be extra irritating.

"Huh?" Mom said.

"*Lydia . . .*" I groaned. Why did she have to just blurt it out like that?

"What? You're going to need a ride to Seattle. So, she may as well know."

"Okay . . . I'm still confused." Mom placed a bandage on my palm.

I glared at Lydia until she read the angry message in my eyes. She slowly backed out of the kitchen and left me alone with Mom.

Suddenly, Mom stopped fussing over my blisters. "Oh! You weren't just training for fun. This was serious."

I nodded.

She held my gaze for a minute. "I get it now. Darren mentioned something about Dominator Ninja during the last physio appointment, didn't he?"

"I wasn't sure you had heard."

"No, no, I heard." Her expression changed, and it seemed as though she had just remembered something. "Oh! I had promised you some equipment . . . Something about a water pit? Sorry, it slipped my mind."

It hadn't slipped *my* mind. I was grateful she had eventually remembered.

"It's like fun summer rehab. Just like Darren said I should do. But it is kind of equipment heavy." At this rate, July would be over before any of the gear even arrived at the house.

"But you need it. It's okay, let me get my computer. We can browse for some things to order for you."

I felt sheepish, but I said, "I have a few things in mind already." There were some items that were just basic ninja equipment — must haves. We'd already managed to get the stumps for free, and I felt lucky to have the best, most expensive item already — the trampoline. But we couldn't make or salvage *everything*. I would have liked more but decided to only ask for the two most important items — a set of hanging rings and a plastic liner for the water pit. This was stuff that wouldn't likely show up in the back of Dad's truck. But then the thought of Dad made me remember something important. "Shouldn't we ask Dad for his permission?"

She looked surprised. "Why would we do that?"

I pressed my lips together. "Nothing. It's nothing." I didn't want to be the reason for another argument, but this was for my wrist. Dad wouldn't get mad, would he?

Mom stared at me over her shoulder before she got up to get her computer. I looked at the bandages across my palms and bent my hands into fists to see how much the bandages got in the way. Looked like tomorrow would be a day for balancing and the trampoline, because these were really going to affect my grip.

Mom opened her laptop. "Okay, let's get you some things you need. Dominator Ninja, for real, huh?" She smiled as she opened the browser window.

After Mom placed the order on Amazon, Lydia said, "Feeding the hungry sharks of corporate greed again?"

"I can't help it if they have the best prices." Mom shrugged. "Come on, it's time for gymnastics."

"Maybe I'll finally get double-jumped." Lydia shot me a look as she picked up her water bottle.

"I'll take Georgia too," Mom told me.

I had to stop myself from openly cheering. I was going to have the house to myself. These rare moments of peace and quiet needed to be cherished and appreciated. I used to just sit in my room and read comics or play games on the iPad, but today, I headed to the backyard.

I surveyed the current layout. I visualized where everything we had just ordered could go. I could ask Dad to put a piece of lumber between two trees at the very back of the yard and we could hang the rings from that. The water pit could go directly under it. It would be awesome. No good ninja course was complete without some kind of high obstacle suspended above a pool of water. A good soaking was a sobering reminder that you hadn't completed the obstacle.

I decided to rearrange the stumps because I needed more challenges. I spaced them out a tiny bit farther than they had been before. Once they were set, I leapt from stump to stump over and over again. When it got easy, I moved the stumps again.

I must have lost track of time, because before I knew it, everybody was back.

"Have you been out here the whole time?" Mom asked from the kitchen window.

"Yeah. I guess so." I wiped my forehead with the back of my hand.

"Come in and take a break. It's getting hot out there. Your face is all red."

"I'm not tired."

"Put a hat on at least." She disappeared from the window and emerged through the back door holding a baseball hat and a glass of water.

As she got closer to me, her nose wrinkled, and she brought her hand up. She held back a laugh. "Ev, you're a huge sweaty mess. A little stinky too."

"I am?" I mean, I felt hot, but it *was* summertime.

I took the glass of water she handed me and downed it in a flash. She put the hat on my head and said, "It's great that you're keeping so active, but everything in moderation. Okay?"

I nodded.

She smiled and said, "You know what? You've inspired me to get back on that stationary bike."

"You mean the laundry rack."

"Ha ha. Funny."

"And when you say 'Get back on,' doesn't that imply that you actually used it before?"

"What a comedian you are today. I did use it! Once!"

"Wasn't that Boxing Day last year?" I teased.

"Gee, aren't you on a roll . . ." Mom tried to look annoyed, but she was suppressing a smile.

"I've got to go ninja some more now." I jerked my head back to my equipment. "You get on that bike."

"I said I was *inspired*. I didn't say I was actually going to *do it*." She turned back toward the house.

"Who's the comedian now?" I asked.

"Come in soon, all right?"

"I will."

But before I came in, I wanted to jump through my stump obstacle one more time. I needed to do it right.

9

THE COURSE TAKES SHAPE

THE PLASTIC LINER WAS GOING TO TAKE MORE than a week to arrive, but the hanging rings arrived in one day. Express overnight shipping is an amazing modern invention. When Dad got home that night and saw them, he wasn't mad about them at all. Must be because he knew it was important that I rehab my wrist. That was good.

That extra lumber he always had piled up in the garage was going to come in handy, and the two trees at the very back of the yard were going to make good anchor points for Dad to assemble everything.

We started the project after dinner. Dad pulled a nail out of his pouch and hammered. "You know, I saw some clips of that Dominator Ninja stuff last night. Looks pretty hard." He shook the piece of lumber to make sure it was secured tightly.

I wasn't sure where he was going with that comment, so I held the wood up like he wanted me to and didn't say anything.

"It's not what I thought at all," he continued.

"What *did* you think? Before?" I asked tentatively. Something about this conversation made me feel a little nervous.

"I thought it was just a bunch of guys scrabbling around, but actually it's pretty impressive."

At last. He finally seemed to understand.

I cleared my throat. "At the end of September, there's a Dominator Ninja event in Seattle. It's a junior edition. What do you think about me trying out for it? We could drive down. Hit the Ivar's?" I tried to hold the piece of wood steady above my head.

He put the hammer down at his side and considered it. "I think that is a great idea." He nodded and a smile crept across his face. "I've always wanted to coach you." He rubbed his left knee while he peeked at the house. Dad lowered his voice. "Because you *are* my only son. I can't let the girls catch me saying stuff like that."

I smiled back. Lydia and Mom would have definitely had something to say if they had heard him.

"I admit I had always hoped it would be a sport like

rugby — you know how much I like rugby. But this bum knee . . ." He flexed it.

I nodded.

"But now that I understand it a bit more, this ninja thing seems not bad." Dad reached up to grab the other end of the piece of wood I was holding so he could nail it in place.

I could hardly believe it — Dad was totally on board! I couldn't stop the sigh of relief. When Dad was done nailing, I closed my eyes. In my mind, I imagined Dad cheering me on from the stands as I stood at the starting line of my first Dominator Ninja: Junior Edition competition. For once, I wasn't going to let him down.

My whole backyard course was coming together quickly. I couldn't just jump on stumps and think that was enough. It wasn't. The rings added a much-needed new element to my training. The blisters on my hands hadn't healed up enough for me to use the rings today, but I could still practice using the climbing holds. They didn't put any pressure on my blisters.

My grip was getting so good now. I didn't have enough of them to climb like I did at Rideau Adventure Playground, but I could hang on to the holds with my fingertips and press my feet against the tree trunk for balance. I felt like a real rock climber.

I could scale it over and over. Just last week I could only hang for five seconds. This week I felt stronger and had more endurance.

"Evan." It was Lydia. Like a cat, she had mastered the art of creeping up on me quietly.

I sighed and climbed down the tree and jumped onto the grass. "What?"

"What *are* you doing?"

"Climbing."

"You've been climbing all morning. I set a timer." She showed me the clock on her iPad ticking away. "One hour and twelve minutes."

I hadn't realized I had been doing this for so long.

"So?"

"I thought this was supposed to be the Summer of Fun."

"It is!"

She scrunched her face. "You and I have very different definitions of *fun*." She walked up to the new set of rings, jumped, and swatted one with her hands before sitting down on a stump.

I sat down on the stump next to her to take a break. I peeled off my bandages, which were just barely hanging on anyway, and examined my raw blisters. "What else would I be doing anyway? I don't have anywhere to be." Mentally,

I counted down the days until the Junior Dominator Ninja event in Seattle. It was only in eleven weeks.

"Okay. I guess. But . . ." She clearly had something more to say but was being careful.

"But what?"

"You're kind of taking this . . . seriously."

I flinched at her words. "So?"

"So, I've just never seen you like this. You're usually pretty *caszh*, you know? Look at your blisters!"

"Maybe it was about time I changed," I said. Being casual never got me anywhere good, did it?

"There was nothing wrong with the old Evan." She shrugged and headed back to the house.

I watched her walk away with her iPad tucked into the crook of her arm.

She may have liked the old Evan, but I didn't. What was there to like? At least now, I was going to be able to say I had my thing. I was going to be a Junior Dominator Ninja, and nobody was going to stop me.

I had to up my game. Using what I could, I made a mini course. I had to start stringing obstacles together. Mastering one obstacle was good, but in Dominator Ninja there was always a string of multiple obstacles to complete.

Because the poles that secured the netting around the trampoline were bendy, I managed to bring the very top of the netting down and tie a piece of fabric to it. When I let go, the net sprang back to its original position, and the fabric was high up. That was going to be my final obstacle. Bounce high enough to grab the fabric. Kind of like capture the flag. It seemed cool to end the course with a flashy move.

Mom came from the house waving the iPad. "Aaron wants to FaceTime!"

"Hey," I said as I took the tablet from Mom.

"Ugh, I'm so bored. How many times can I paddle in this annoying canoe with my uncle?" I could see he was sitting on a dock with some water behind him. It looked pretty decent. "What are you doing?"

"Well, remember that picture of the trampoline I sent you?"

"Yes! That sucks that I'm not there to enjoy it!" It hadn't been that long since I'd seen him, but he looked tanned. His freckles seemed to have multiplied in the Ontario sunshine.

"I know. But you can use it in a little while."

"I'm here until the end of August." Aaron rolled his eyes.

"Hey, you know what? I got even more stuff in the backyard now."

"You got even more stuff! No fair!"

"Let me show you!" I was nervous and excited to see his reaction. "I have a . . . ninja course set up now." He stood up. "What? For real? Show me! Show me!" I could see that he wasn't wearing a shirt, just swim trunks. Cottage life seemed very relaxed.

"It's just my first one, so it can change and be flexible, but right now it's set up so I start on the stumps. See?" I bounced from stump to stump to show him.

"Then I scale up all these climbing holds." I panned the iPad from the lowest hold to the highest one.

"Cool! Like your own personal rock wall! I mean tree wall!"

"Then these." I walked over to the rings and showed him.

"Yeah, you totally need a bunch of different obstacles back-to-back. I've seen it on TV."

Aaron understood perfectly.

"After, I do the rings — for now, I have to pretend like there's a water pit under them. The plastic liner we need to make it hasn't arrived yet."

"WHAT? You're going to get a water pit too!" Aaron's eyes were bulging.

"Then, I run to the trampoline, jump, and grab the flag." I lifted the iPad up high so he could see the flag I had attached to very top of the netting.

"That is so cool!"

I smiled. It *was* cool.

"I was . . ." He heard somebody calling for him off the screen and turned to look at them. Aaron sighed and hung his head. His hair was getting so long his shaggy brown bangs covered his eyes. "They want me to get a campfire going to roast our chicken and potatoes for dinner. I'm practically an expert at lighting kindling."

It seemed to be too early to be thinking about dinner. But he was three hours ahead. "Funny, I haven't even had lunch yet."

"Campfires are *not* a time-efficient way to cook."

"Okay. Thanks for calling. You go light your fire. It was good to catch up. I've got to go practice anyway."

"Later." Aaron waved at the screen. I waved back and ended the call.

I had just put the iPad down when a notification dinged.

It was from Aaron again.

Forgot to say glad u found something cool to do wrist must be 100%! That's awesome. Suddenly, I felt good about *everything* — even my wrist.

10

THE KLUTZ IS BACK

AFTER TALKING TO AARON, I FELT A SURGE OF energy. There was no better time than the present to actually practice the course. Start to finish. For real. From inside the house, I retrieved my watch with a timer. I also got a pad of paper from the kitchen to start keeping track of my progress.

Finishing a course was important, but so was finishing the course quickly. I wanted to see improvement each time. I made a little chart and in the first box, added today's date: July 16. The summer was just flying by. I didn't have much time left to train. According to the last update, the plastic liner hadn't even shipped yet!

When everything was set up, I stood in front of the first stump and held my finger against the start button on my watch. I puffed out some air before I pressed the button and took off.

I raced through all the obstacles as quickly as I could. I practically flew across the rings, and if my skin under my blisters hurt, I didn't even feel it. I was in some kind of zone of awesomeness. By the time I scrambled up to the trampoline, my eyes zoomed in on the flag waiting for me at the top of the netting. I bounced as high as I could, but I missed. I bounced again and stretched with everything I had.

I grabbed the flag and yanked at it. But it snagged. I didn't want to let go of the flag and the flag didn't want to let go of the net. The net bent, like it was supposed to, but it pushed me off balance. Before I knew what was happening, I got twisted in the air.

I felt my ribs crunching on top of my right wrist and forearm as I landed hard. On the rebound, I rolled to the left, so that on the next bounce I wouldn't come down on my wrist again. When the trampoline finally stopped tossing me around, I had the flag in my hand, but I knew what had happened. I had hurt my wrist again.

"The doctor said it was just a sprain. He's seen worse."

"Just when I thought I was recovered." I was still feeling numb from the news.

"It will get better. Just like last time."

I ignored Mom's attempts at trying to make me feel better. At the moment, sulking was the only thing I had the energy for.

"Come on, Ev. Don't mope around. It's not the end of the world."

"I'm allowed to sulk. My plans have been ruined."

"Oh, the ninja plans?" Mom murmured.

"It was the *only* plan I had."

"You can still do it," she said brightly.

"I'm out two, three weeks! There are only about ten weeks left before the event." I hung my head. "I don't have enough time to practice. I don't want to show up at an event unprepared. That would be humiliating. It's just not going to happen now. There's no time."

"Okay, maybe you're right about that. But *next year* is definitely an option." Mom kept trying to sound chipper.

"But it won't be in Seattle then. I saw on the website that it will be in Portland then."

Lydia glanced at me from the other sofa. "Portland is not as close as Seattle, but still definitely within driving distance." She returned to her iPad.

I just ignored her. Portland was farther in space *and* time. I had had my heart set on Seattle *this year*, not Portland next year. I was going to surprise Darren. I choked out a bitter laugh.

"Okay. You probably need some alone time. I'll get out of your hair." Mom stood up and left.

Unlike Mom, my sisters couldn't take a hint. I wished they would just get lost. Georgia approached. She hovered over me briefly, oblivious to my need for solitude, before she gently slapped my face.

I batted her hand away.

"Ehbun." Georgia stared at me intensely.

"Oh, go away." I turned away from her and pulled the throw blanket over me. "Evan needs Sulking Time."

"What's Sulking Time?"

"That's when a loser's summer plans get ruined, and he needs time to get over it. I might be here a while."

"Don't call yourself bad things!" She gently shoved my back.

"Why not? It's true."

Georgia put her head down on the side of my ribs.

"Train with me," she said in a creepy whisper voice.

I shifted my position to look at her.

"How on earth can I train with *you*? You're still in pull-ups."

"Don't shame her, you jerk," Lydia hissed. "Your bad mood does not give you the right to be disrespectful."

I wasn't exactly in the mood to be lectured by Lydia right now, but she was right.

"Sorry, Georgia." I patted her head. "I wasn't being nice."

She climbed on top of me and sat down on my stomach.

I let out a small *oof.*

"That's okay. I know you're wrong." Nonchalantly, she

picked at an old crusty grain of rice, stuck to her leggings.

I looked at her, puzzled. I thought it was best to keep my mouth shut and hope this whole conversation fizzled out.

"I like for you to read books to me. I like funny Ehbun." She lifted the blanket and slapped my leg.

What did *that* mean? Was I just her personal audiobook narrator?

"Let's go get a treat!" Mom said. "Ice cream? Should we get ice cream?"

Bribing with sugar. An age-old parental distraction technique.

"Gelato," Lydia said. "That place with eight hundred and fifty flavors made by the guy who won some competition in Italy."

I perked up. Not only did that shop have 850 flavors, but also it was named 850 Gelato. I smacked my lips together. I might get up off the sofa for 850 Gelato.

"It's a bit far away," Mom said.

Lydia stared at her. "What? Are we busy?"

When Dad came home, Georgia raced up, tugged at his leg, and announced, "I picked ginger and lemon!"

Dad looked at her, confused. "Are you fighting off a cold?"

"No, silly! It's July! To eat!"

"Okay . . ." Dad tried to make sense of what Georgia was talking about. "I guess that sounds very healthy!"

He was so confused by Georgia's conversation that it took him a while to notice the wrap I had on my wrist.

When he did, his face changed noticeably.

"What happened?" He eyed me up and down.

"I hurt it. Again."

"What do you mean?"

"I . . . landed funny."

His shoulders sagged as he looked at me. I braced myself, waiting to hear what he was going to say about me. *Klutz. Clumsy. Awkward.* Something like that.

But instead, he said to Mom, "How did you let this happen?"

She stiffened. "It was an accident."

"What do you even do all day if you don't keep an eye on your kids?"

It didn't seem fair that he was blaming *her* because of what I had done. This was all on *me*. My stomach twisted in knots.

Georgia, who had moved to the coffee table, slammed her sippy cup down. "Mommy's busy!"

"Like you've never had an injury before . . ." Lydia glared at Dad and dropped her eyes down to his left knee.

"Well still, this is bad news. How are you going to train?" Dad rubbed his forehead.

As if I hadn't been wondering the same thing.

"It's just a small sprain," I spoke up. "Doctor said I should rest it for a couple of weeks."

Dad's nostrils flared as he eyed me up and down. "No climbing or hanging, probably, right?"

I nodded.

"Well, I guess you're never going to win now."

"Dinner," Mom said abruptly. She practically pushed me to the table.

I was glad Mom was an expert at using food to change the topic. I didn't want to talk about what I couldn't and wouldn't be able to do anymore.

We started to gather around the table. Mom scooped out small bowls of rice while Lydia got glasses of water for everybody. I sat down miserably and stared at my chopsticks.

Not this again. This injured wrist kept forcing me to change my normal habits. Just like at the gelato shop, when I normally would have ordered a scoop in a cup with one of those small, brightly colored spoons, today I had had to order a scoop in a cone and was forced to lick. I hate licking. It's like continuously eating your own saliva. But for 850 Gelato's strawberry and Valrhona chocolate, I was willing to compromise.

Now, when we were having Korean food for dinner, there was only one logical utensil choice — chopsticks. Picking up kimchi with a *fork*? That's just *wrong*. Uncivilized, even. I'd already lived like that *before*. I did not want to have to live like that again. But here I was.

I tried picking the chopsticks up with my heavily bandaged right wrist but gave up immediately. It was no good. I just couldn't hold them.

I got up to grab a fork from the cutlery drawer. Just call me Evan, the Rude.

"Oh, sorry. I forgot," Mom said.

"Well, Ev, looks like this whole ninja thing was a total fail." Dad scooped some rice into his mouth.

My cheeks flushed.

"There's always Portland," Lydia said quietly. "You were doing great. I saw." She gave my back a quick pat. "For real." She tossed some pieces of kimchi into my bowl and side-eyed me.

I *had* been doing great. When I stared down at my wrist, my thoughts immediately went back to the rehab room at Kids Only Physio. Would I end up back there learning how to use chopsticks all over again?

I wanted to kick myself. I didn't want to go back to see Darren *there*, because the only place I wanted to see him again was in *Seattle* at Dominator Ninja.

Tightly, I gripped my fork in my left hand. Something in my chest burned. *Total fail.* Dad wasn't just talking about ninja stuff; he was talking about me.

11

MUDDY DETOUR

OVER THE NEXT TWO DAYS, I MOSTLY SAT ON THE sofa with Mom's laptop battery overheating on top of my legs. I tried not to watch any more Dominator Ninja videos, but YouTube kept recommending them to me. I finally selected the "Not Interested" option in one of the thumbnail previews, hoping they would stop showing up.

It worked. But instead, they started recommending something called Soiled Pants races. The logo looked kind of familiar. I think I had seen it on a bumper sticker on a car once.

I clicked on one of the videos, because what else did I have going on? The Summer of Fun? Ha. Not so far. More like the Summer of Extreme Frustration. I had nothing but time, and we had an unlimited internet plan.

Soiled Pants was an outdoor obstacle course race held in a big field that was super muddy. The main color of the videos was a medium tan — the course and all the people in it. Everything was coated in mud.

It was a race where everybody on a team had to complete one obstacle in a series, like a relay. If somebody failed their obstacle, the whole team failed. There's a lot of pressure to succeed. Nobody wants to let their whole team down. I watched a celebrity race from last year.

I found myself laughing hysterically. I wasn't sure if it was genuinely funny or if I just had this pent up need to laugh, but watching these famous singers and actors go *splat* in the mud was exactly what I needed.

Lydia joined me on the sofa and started watching too. "Is this what you've been laughing about?"

Together we watched somebody try to run across a log while being pelted by balls. They slipped and they landed with the log between their legs.

"Oh!" Lydia and I both gasped. Then we started laughing. I think he was a rapper, but I couldn't recognize him with his entire body covered in mud and his face contorted in agony. I should have felt some sympathy for the poor guy, but because it wasn't me, all I did was laugh my head off.

The race continued. The commentator on the video said, "This obstacle. A classic Soiled Pants event. *Boulder over the Shoulder!* A true test of strength and grit!"

"*Boulder over the Shoulder!*" Georgia giggled. Her picture books had trained her to become addicted to rhymes. She had climbed up onto the back of the sofa and was watching too.

We watched a well-known news announcer hoist a rock onto her shoulder. Geez, she was impressive. You never would have guessed she was going to be so ferocious. She growled as she carried the rock across the finish line.

"You go, girl!" Georgia shouted.

When the race was done, Lydia asked, "Where *was* that video from?"

"Dirty ninja?" Georgia asked.

"No, it wasn't a ninja event. It was Soiled Pants: Celebrity Edition."

"That was too funny." Lydia wiped a tear from her eye.

"Looks like dirty ninjas!" Georgia said.

"Stop calling it dirty ninja! It's not the same at all!" I felt offended. How could she not see that the two were completely different!

"What do you mean? It's totally like dirty ninja." Lydia laughed. "Let me guess, YouTube's algorithm suggested the video for you, right?"

I didn't even know what an algorithm *was*.

"It predicted you'd like it, because AI is scary like that."

"YouTube isn't all-powerful, okay? They're totally different. First of all, Soiled Pants is *grimy*," I said scowling. "You know how Dominator Ninja is done at night with all that bright lighting and cool equipment? Secondly, it's a *team* event. Dominator Ninja is just you and the course."

Lydia shrugged. "Just a different kind of fun, if you ask me."

"Mud is funner!" Georgia declared. "Having teammates is fun, too!"

I stared at my little sister. What did she know?

Lydia picked Georgia up and tossed her over her shoulder, just like the news anchor tossed the boulder in the race. "You're a toddler on my shoulder! I'm heading to the finish line! *Grrr!*" She snarled and sprinted down the hallway while the two of them giggled.

"See! Teams are fun!" Georgia yelled.

The next day, after spending most of the day sitting on the sofa watching a *SpongeBob SquarePants* marathon on TV while my right arm dangled uselessly by my side, I finally got tired of it and decided to send a message to Aaron and Davey. They'd sympathize with me — wouldn't they?

I pecked out a message in a group chat with the index finger of my left hand. I attached a photo of my bandaged wrist.

Aren't I lucky?

Davey answered immediately. **What happened??!!!?**

I fell. Cuz I'm a big L

Three bubbles pulsed as Davey typed. **Rough but just an accident. Not broken again right?**

Not

I felt Mom glaring at me as I stared at the screen. I turned around to look at her.

"Get outside." Her expression was stern.

"Why? I'm fine where I am."

"You're sucking the oxygen from the room."

"I have to *breathe*."

She crossed her arms in front of her chest and flared her nostrils. "It was a metaphor. Let me rephrase. You're still mopey. It's irritating. At least you turned off the TV. SpongeBob's laugh is ringing in my ears."

"I don't want to go outside." My right wrist wasn't throbbing anymore, but it wasn't up to doing anything physical. I didn't even want to look at the hanging rings or the climbing holds.

"Too bad. Go." She pointed her finger and stared at me until I moved.

Boss says I gotta go.

Breakfast time for me anyway. Talk later.

I put down the iPad and got up off the sofa. "Okay, okay. Geez." I muttered.

At the back door, I slipped into some sandals. Because I was forced to be here, the only thing I decided I could do was take a nap on the trampoline. I put my head down and thought about Davey's message. *Just an accident.* Sure, he was right, but still, why did accidents have to keep happening to me?

12

THE DOUBLE JUMP

I TRIED TO GET COMFORTABLE ON THE TRAMPOLINE, but I just couldn't. Instead, I brooded about my bad luck. Speaking of bad luck, it had only been a few minutes since Mom ejected me from the house and there they were, ready to start harassing me already — my sisters.

"Is Ehbun have Sulking Time on trampoline?" Georgia asked Lydia. She waddled outside, holding Lydia's hand.

"At least he got off the couch," Lydia said.

"I'm not sulking. I'm trying to take a nap."

"Georgia nap, too!"

Lydia helped Georgia up and then zipped the two of us in together, like animals locked in a cage.

"Gee, thanks," I said to Lydia. "Just what I needed."

"Just what Georgia needs, too!" Georgia curled up next to me and used me like a pillow. "It's nap time!"

Lydia pulled a fresh stick of gum out of the pocket of her hoodie before she climbed up to join us.

Georgia snuggled up to me. "*Shhh*, quiet time," she said sleepily.

"Good grief." I was trapped.

"Hey! I want to show you something," Lydia said quietly. Somehow Georgia had fallen asleep in exactly twenty seconds.

"What?" I asked.

Lydia held the iPad in front of me and she gently sat down.

SOILED PANTS
REGULAR TEAM EVENT AND FAMILY EDITION

For the first time, Soiled Pants will be setting up in Vancouver! Join us on the last weekend . of summer for a weekend of fun.

⇥ TWO DAYS OF COMPETITIONS! ⇤

⏵ DAY 1: FAMILY EDITION ⏴

Family Edition is a modified event
so you can compete with families of all ages!

⏵ DAY 2: REGULAR TEAM EVENT ⏴

Both days, the top three teams will receive medals.
Cool, but here's the best part:

*All participants who finish the race will receive a chance to
win a one-year free family membership to the all-new Agile
Ninja Training Centre. Practice on the latest and greatest
obstacle course facility in the area. Not as muddy there as
we like but save time and money on laundry!*

TEST YOUR FORTITUDE WITH EVENTS LIKE*:

➤➤ Clunky Monkey Bars

➤➤ Mucky Mud Pit

➤➤ Sticky Spiderweb Net

➤➤ Boulder over the Shoulder

➤➤ Dodge the Log

➤➤ Storm the Wall

REQUIREMENTS: AN APPETITE FOR MUD AND A HEART FULL OF GRIT.

*PLEASE NOTE: THIS LIST IS SUBJECT TO CHANGE

AND DEPENDS ON LOCAL CONDITIONS.

⫤ Register now to secure your spot. ⫣

After reading it, I passed the iPad back to Lydia without saying anything.

"So?" Lydia asked. "What do you think?"

I shrugged indifferently. "Why are you on the Soiled Pants website anyway?"

She smiled. "The videos we saw earlier were funny. I was just investigating."

"*Family* edition," I said scornfully.

"What's with the tone?" Lydia asked.

"All ages? You know what *that* means."

"No, I don't know what *that* means," Lydia retorted.

"That means it's *easy*. That means Georgia could do it." I looked down at my sleeping sister.

"Georgia do?" Her eyes popped opened, and she rubbed them with the back of her hand.

"Look at these pictures." Lydia leaned over and swiped the screen, showing different photos from previous family races. "Does *this* look easy to you?"

The pictures seemed to show people in various levels of distress and filth. Unlike the celebrity edition I had seen, these pictures had a lot of teenagers and even some really young kids, like Georgia. It sort of did look fun, I had to admit.

"Okay, maybe it's not *completely* easy, but you forgot. One major problem." I flashed her my bandaged wrist.

"Okay, you couldn't do the monkey bars part, but you could definitely do something called *Mucky Mud Pit*, even with a slightly injured wrist, couldn't you? Looks like you just wade your way through the mud."

"I guess . . ."

"So, what do you think?" Lydia asked.

I didn't say anything. Mostly because I didn't know what to think. I was still extremely bummed out from not being able to train for this year's Dominator Ninja. Training to wade through mud didn't seem exactly . . . *inspiring*.

Lydia looked disappointed. "Oh. I thought it looked kind of fun."

"I didn't say that it didn't look fun."

"But you don't look very enthusiastic, either." She held the iPad limply and the screen went dark.

"It's hard to have enthusiasm for anything when your wrist aches, okay?"

"But it's not always going to hurt. While it recovers, couldn't you . . . change your focus a little? Maybe we could do this event . . . with you. All together?" Lydia asked shyly. "If you look at some of these pictures" — she lifted the iPad again — "a lot of teams wear custom T-shirts. Wouldn't it be funny if we all wore black tees that said 'Team Park' in big letters across the back? We'd be known as that tough Korean-Canadian family." She chuckled.

I snorted. Lydia's arms were about as thick as spaghettini noodles, and Georgia was just a little toddler with legs that looked like baguettes. Not exactly a family that made you cross the street if you saw them coming in your direction.

"Have you seen the regular Soiled Pants event? Not just the celebrity edition?" she asked.

I shook my head.

"Look." Lydia started a video clip.

We watched a race, from start to finish. We cringed. We held our collective breath. We laughed. We cheered.

"Wait," Lydia said, as the race we watched came to an end. "This is the best part."

By the end, all the participants were absolutely filthy, and covered in a layer of mud, but I noticed that every single person had a big smile on their face. Their white teeth really stood out against all the mud.

I found myself anxiously waiting to see what was next. Everybody walked over to . . . *hoses*? At the end, the contestants sprayed each other clean with water. There was screaming and yelling. Kind of like a celebration.

It wasn't a confetti bomb exactly, but still, everybody was having a blast. If you sprayed the hose straight up into the air, it came down like *wet* confetti. Or at least a close approximation. I glanced over at Lydia and Georgia and wondered exactly how good it would feel to spray water in their faces without worrying about getting into trouble.

Lydia said, "We could have so much fun!"

"Wait, are you actually interested in doing this?" I asked.

"I'm interested if *you're* interested."

"You'd do this" — I pointed to the picture on the screen with a girl who was doing a face-plant in the mud — "for *me*?"

"I'd do anything for my Evey Wevey," Lydia said in a baby voice.

"Lydyah funny." Georgia started rolling around on the trampoline.

"Why'd you have to go and ruin a perfectly nice moment?" I asked.

"Let's not get too sappy here." She shoved my shoulder gently.

"Agreed."

"I know it's not what you wanted. I know you wanted your *thing*. Your solo thing. But you can always have your thing. Just maybe a year later than you thought. If we end up driving to Portland next year, we still take the same highway we'd take if we drove to Seattle. We just go a bit farther south. Just think! We'll pass by even more American drive-thrus." Lydia smacked her lips together. "So, *this* year, we could do this instead." She tapped the iPad. "Think about it?"

"Okay, I'll think about it." I twisted my mouth. I did like American drive-thrus, but they'd always be there. Even next year.

But for this year, I had to admit, there was something sort of homey about an event that involved mud, ropes, and logs. It wasn't as cool as Dominator Ninja — no giant plexiglass wheels or flashing neon signs, but it was something. A different kind of fun.

I still had to wrap my mind around the *family* part, though. What it meant was I had to just do *one* part of the race. The rest was up to *them*. I eyed Lydia and Georgia.

That was the one constant about family — annoying siblings never giving you any space. I could try to fight it, or I could just accept it. Then it struck me. They weren't even the problem. *Mom and Dad*. What were *they* going to say about it? Reality started to set in.

"I don't think Mom and Dad are going to go for it," I told Lydia.

She considered me for a minute. "Okay, I admit, maybe Mom will be a hard sell, but let me worry about that. Dad, on the other hand. Are you kidding? He'll be all over the idea of 'getting back out there.'" Lydia used finger quotes.

I nodded. Dad *had* been super into it when he tried jumping on the stumps.

"Daddy likes to win!" Georgia agreed.

Lydia brought the iPad closer to her and started typing. "He'll be super excited at the prospect of a medal to put in the cabinet." She grinned. "I'm signing us up!"

I didn't say no. I didn't stop her. Because I had to admit, I was getting into this whole idea too. At first, I was pretty devastated about reinjuring my wrist, and it was clear that

I didn't have enough time to train for this year's event in Seattle. But, on the plus side, the side I hadn't been able to see until just now, waiting until next year's event only meant one thing: more time to practice. Darren would be in Portland next year too, I'd bet money on it.

By then, my hands would be calloused and tough like Lydia's. That took time and a lot of hard work. Time is what I had. Plus, if we managed to complete the Soiled Pants race, we had a chance for a free membership to the Agile Ninja Training Centre. I didn't even know that there was such a place! That sounded pretty good. Awesome, even. If I could train at that gym, who knows how good I could get! Getting a medal would be pretty nice too, even if I had to share it with my family.

It seemed like Soiled Pants: Family Edition was a win-win situation. I'd be able to get a competition under my belt — get my feet wet. Or should I say, get my feet *dirty*? I would just have to find one event I was strong in. One event I could do with a wrist that was still on the mend.

"Registration done!" Lydia said.

I nodded. "Okay. Let's do this."

It looked like I was going to soil my pants — in a *good* way, not the ultra-embarrassing way that would force me to become a hermit.

I stretched and twisted my body.

Lydia hopped out of the trampoline and put her iPad down on the ground before she climbed back in and started jumping. Georgia and I bounced around on our bums. "Now, would you double-jump me already?" Lydia started bouncing. "I feel like I've been waiting *forever* for this!"

I got up and started bouncing too.

"Sulking Time all done!" Georgia squealed.

"I guess so." I suddenly felt lighter. "Move to the side, Georgia." I pumped my legs at just the right time and sent Lydia flying high.

I watched Lydia reach an almost unbelievable height. Lydia could easily jump high on her own, but when I helped her, she soared — maybe we all needed other people to help us reach farther than we could on our own.

13

RECRUITING, PHASE 1

THE THREE OF US SPENT THE AFTERNOON SITTING on the trampoline watching more Soiled Pants highlights. The events looked pretty consistent. For me, I was focusing on events where the participants used mostly leg strength or speed.

Mucky Mud Pit. It had to be my event. It was mostly just power walking through deep mud.

But I kept feeling uneasy about the rest of the obstacles. Lydia could pretty much tackle anything. Dad was old, but he was naturally pretty tough and had the right mindset to overcome stiff joints and difficult tasks. I wasn't worried about them. *Georgia.* Ugh. *Mom.* Double ugh.

After a lot of deep thought, I told Lydia, "There's nothing here that looks like something Mom could do." I dusted away choco pie crumbs from my lap.

"Yeah, she's going to have to . . ." Lydia paused.

"Work," I said. "She's totally out of shape."

"Her shape is round," Georgia said. She sipped her box of soy milk.

"Did you just say that in a judge-y way?" Lydia looked shocked. "So what if she's round? Wow, it's truly disappointing how young we learn biases!" Lydia began to lecture. "Listen, kid, you have got to listen to me."

"Georgia is a good listener." She leaned in.

"Everybody has a different body. There is no *good* body shape or *bad* body shape. We're just worried that Mom is . . ." Lydia struggled to find the right word.

"Weak with no muscles?" I suggested. "If she doesn't get fitter, she might die out in the field." I showed Georgia pictures from the race where people were lying down in the mud. It didn't seem like they were going to get up.

Georgia's eyes grew wide. She leaned in closer to the screen. "Dying in mud is not fun."

"Everybody's body looks different. But they are all *good*."

"Different bodies," Georgia agreed. "All good."

Lydia patted Georgia's head. "You got it, right?"

"Okay, now use that enthusiasm and convince Mom

to get on that stationary bike she never uses or some-thing," I said.

"The bike!" Lydia smiled. "I have to *spin* it just right to convince her."

I did a face palm because Lydia looked a little too pleased with herself.

"Georgia's good at spinning." She stood up, extended her arms to the side, and started whirling herself around.

"Let's just try to convince her how much fun it could be," I told Lydia as I watched Georgia spin herself dizzy.

Georgia finally fell down and looked to the sky. "Mud tastes delicious!"

"I'm afraid to ask how you know," I said.

"From before . . ."

"I'll take your word for it."

"Go Peloton!" Georgia raised a fist.

"I think she may watch too much TV," Lydia said to me as we laughed in disbelief.

Newly invigorated, I couldn't stop thinking about ways to train for Soiled Pants. It was actually not that different from ninja training. The more videos I watched, the more I realized there were a lot of similarities. It *was* like dirty ninja.

A lot of climbing (not for me), a lot of jumping (definitely doable), some strenuous lifting (Dad's domain), and a lot of possibilities for falling (my area of expertise, apparently). In a ninja course, you fell onto a soft mat or a water pit. In a Soiled Pants race, you fell into mud.

Unlike Georgia, I had very little experience with mud. I typed "How to make a good mud pit" into Google. There was surprisingly little information on how to make the kind of mud that was good for obstacle courses.

But after a bit more searching, something very interesting came up. I realized a mud pit was basically the same thing as a water pit, like the kind I had wanted for a ninja course. It was just filled with a different material! The plastic liner was going to come in handy. I needed to check its shipping status. It seemed like it was arriving on the world's slowest freighter.

Excited with this idea, I got up from the deck chair and walked back to the trampoline.

"Hey guys," I said to my sisters.

Lydia stopped jumping. "No *guys* here, except you."

I sighed. "I'm sorry. How about, excuse me, Lydia and Georgia?"

"Yes, how may we help you?" Lydia replied innocently.

"What do you think about this?" I showed them a picture from a website called *Totally Radical Mud Adventures*.

Lydia laughed. "Oh my god. I love it."

I pointed to the spot in the yard where I had originally imagined the water pit. "It can go right there."

Georgia was given clear instructions to keep her mouth shut. She curled her lips between her teeth to remind herself.

Mom was sitting on the sofa, folding laundry. "You three have been outside for a long time! I knew that trampoline was going to be a lot of fun for you."

"It's great!" Lydia said.

I nudged her to get her talking, like we had planned.

"Do you have personal fitness goals for this summer, by any chance?" Lydia asked.

Mom put the towel she was folding down on her lap.

"To make sure I only wear elastic-waist pants."

Lydia fake laughed. "Those *are* the best kind of pants. I mean . . . while the three of us are busy outside, giving you the gift of time, I thought it might be a wonderful idea for you to finally take up the stationary bike trend. Since we already have one."

Mom frowned slightly. "I'm busy."

I stepped up. "Just wondering. Do you know when the plastic water pit liner you ordered will arrive?"

"I got a notification that it would arrive by next Tuesday afternoon. You don't want me to return it already, do you?"

"No! No! Not at all! In fact, I was wondering if we might . . . do a little job before it arrives." I watched Mom's expression carefully.

"Dig a mud pit!" Georgia exclaimed. She immediately clamped her hand over her mouth, looked at me, and sat down. She tucked her lips between her teeth again. Not that it had done any good the first time.

"Dig a mud pit?" Mom asked. She was starting to get that suspicious look in her eyes.

Lydia sat down next to Mom and picked up a pair of leggings to fold.

"Mom," she said in a hushed tone. She glared at me, and I sat down and picked up a shirt. "You know how Evan was *super* disappointed about reinjuring his wrist."

I grimaced as I put a badly folded shirt on top of the pile.

Lydia continued, "We found a really great opportunity for him to . . ."

"Dirty ninja!" Georgia slammed her hand to her mouth again.

Lydia made an angry face in Georgia's direction.

I watched Mom's lips as they started to pucker noticeably.

Lydia collected her thoughts. "Mom. Do you know about Soiled Pants?"

Mom tilted her head. "I'm a bit of an expert. All three of you have soiled your pants at some point."

I held back a laugh.

"Ha ha. Good one. But I mean Soiled Pants, the *obstacle* course race." Lydia managed to keep sounding pleasant, despite just being roasted.

"Oh, the *race*. Sounds kind of familiar."

"Do you want to see?" Lydia asked, tapping her iPad.

While Mom watched, I matched socks. What an annoying task. Why did everybody wear white ankle socks? Mom stopped folding and silently watched the clip Lydia played for her. Georgia climbed onto her lap and watched too.

"Ouch!" Mom grimaced.

When the clip was over, Mom picked up a pair of pants. "That looks fun."

"Oh, I'm so glad you think so!" Lydia said with extra enthusiasm.

I watched Mom's face, like a lightbulb flickering to life, as she sat up and asked, "Why did you just show me that?"

"Oh, my wrist needs some ice . . ." I moaned quietly. I held it gingerly as I headed to the refrigerator. Very lightly, I touched the corner of my Summer of Fun poster, still taped to the refrigerator. The confetti, the Space Needle — those things weren't going to happen now. But maybe I should find a brown crayon and shade the picture with mud instead. It could still be the Summer of Fun, with a small, mucky detour.

"Evan was just *crushed* about not being able to train for this year's Junior Dominator Ninja. Maybe even more than you realized." Lydia lowered her voice, but I could still hear her from the kitchen.

I glanced back toward the living room. Mom held Lydia's gaze.

"You know how important it was for him to try to find his own *thing*." She lifted her chin and gestured toward the glass IKEA display cabinet.

When she did that, I felt a small flush rise on my neck. It was *true*, but I didn't exactly enjoy the reminder.

"There's not enough time for him to really make a good go of it for this year's ninja thing, but this Soiled Pants family race would be a nice substitute, don't you think? Until his wrist heals up again."

While I rummaged around the freezer drawer, I made sure to make a lot of noise.

"But we have to do it *with* him. It's the only way right now. We can do that for him, can't we, Mom?" Lydia batted her eyes.

"Show me another clip," Mom said.

Lydia tapped the screen and Mom watched silently. I placed an ice pack on my wrist and stood by the kitchen counter. Lydia glanced up to meet my gaze and raised her eyebrows in my direction before resuming her somber expression.

After watching the clip, Mom wilted into the sofa. "You want *me* to do *that*?" she whispered to Lydia.

Georgia slapped Mom's thigh. "You can do it!"

Mom nodded. "Okay, for Evan."

She was in. Lydia helped Mom finish all the laundry silently. From my spot in the kitchen, I couldn't see Lydia's face clearly, but I imagined she was feeling quite pleased with herself.

When Mom got up to take the laundry upstairs, Georgia shouted, "Double time! Faster! Faster!" She pushed Mom up the stairs.

"Okay!" Mom said. "Eat my dust!"

I cringed. Wow, Mom was *slow*. We were really going to have to do something about that.

"Most reluctant member recruited," Lydia muttered as she walked by me in the kitchen.

"You're kind of scary," I told Lydia.

"Scary *impressive*, right?"

I chuckled silently. "What are we going to tell Dad?" I asked. It was late afternoon, and he would be home soon.

"I've got this." Lydia seemed sure of herself. "I'm definitely joining the Debate Team in the spring. I've got a taste for the power of a persuasive argument." Lydia plunked herself down on the sofa.

I had no doubt she would win any debate she wanted to. When she started adding debate prizes to her gymnastics medals, her shelf in the IKEA cabinet would soon be overflowing. Dad would be proud, in his way. But, I wasn't ready to give her *my* shelf space — not yet. With a little help, I hoped we could walk away from the Soiled Pants race with a little hardware. Not exactly *mine* but something I had been part of. Played a key role in achieving it, even.

And then next year, maybe, when my wrist was strong, who knows what else I could do. Especially if I could join a real ninja gym and train properly with the right equipment.

Then maybe Dad would stop seeing what *wasn't* in the cabinet on my shelf space and start seeing me.

14

RECRUITING, PHASE 2

LYDIA RUSHED OUTSIDE TO TALK TO DAD THE minute he came home. From the kitchen, I strained to hear something, *anything*, but couldn't. All I could see was that Dad was listening intently. Then Lydia pulled out her iPad.

After a few seconds, he nodded, and they walked into the house together. I pretended to be casually flipping through the weekly bundle of flyers. Looked like ground beef and field tomatoes were on sale this week.

"Hey," Dad announced. "I'm just going to be in the backyard for a bit. Call me when dinner's ready."

"What did you say to him?" I asked.

"All the right things." Lydia kicked off her shoes and grinned.

"What's he doing?" I asked. I peered out the kitchen window. Mom joined me.

Dad had a measuring tape and was scribbling something down on a pad of paper.

"Oh no, he's doing measurements. You know how he gets with measurements," Mom said. "I'd better hurry and distract him with food."

She returned to the kitchen to finish dinner preparations.

Georgia was sitting on the floor, deeply engrossed in setting up figures in a line. Lydia joined her. They quietly continued to set up wooden blocks so they snaked around the family room.

"You're not going to tell me anything?" I asked Lydia.

She glanced over her shoulder mysteriously. "Let's just say, he's all in."

Georgia held a small figurine, a raggedy doll, no bigger than her hand, and placed it on the block. "Jump faster!" she exclaimed as she helped the doll jump from block to block.

The desire to complete an obstacle course was contagious. Even the toys in this house were training.

Dad didn't come in right away. I heard some banging outside, and when I peeked to see what he was doing, he had driven four stakes into the ground. Now, he was starting to wrap a strand of twine around one of the stakes before pulling the string to the next stake. He had just laid out a rectangle.

"He's not wasting any time, is he?" Lydia asked from her spot on the floor next to Georgia.

"What *is* he doing?" I asked.

Dad finally came in just as Mom was starting to put out plates.

"So?" Lydia asked. "Doable?"

Dad nodded. "Yup. This weekend, we dig."

"You're going to get your mud pit!" Lydia beamed.

My mouth fell open. "Really?"

"I'm looking forward to all of us getting our competitive juices going. I realized how long it has been since this old Park let out a bark!" He howled.

I startled. It was truly a weird experience watching Dad pretend he was a wolf, or a coyote, or whatever it was he was doing.

"Daddy funny!" Georgia raced up to him and grabbed his leg. "Usually only serious and boring!"

He picked her up and swung her around. "A little competition is exactly what everybody needs!" Dad looked genuinely excited.

Mom sighed heavily, and she put down plates around the table.

"Team Park!" Dad yelled.

➤➤ ➤➤ ➤➤

The following Saturday morning, Team Park stood in a line in our backyard. Dad had brought home a little excavator on a trailer yesterday and everybody just expected him to get in and start digging, but instead, he reached into the cab and, from next to the seat, he pulled out a roll of paper.

"Here's our plan for today." Dad was all business as he unrolled a drawing and used rocks on the corners to keep the paper flat.

"Detailed *drawings*?" Mom took one look at them and rolled her eyes. "So fast?"

He glared at her. "You need a plan for this kind of thing. You've got to do it right."

Every time they talked to each other like this, I got a sticky, lumpy feeling in my throat.

I glanced over at Lydia, and our eyes met briefly. She looked away and I could see her thinking.

"Oh sure, the drawings might *seem* unnecessary, but if we run into any difficulties, they could be very useful," Lydia said.

Dad seemed to lift his chin a bit higher, but Mom's face turned into a distinct scowl.

"I'll dig as much as I can with the machine, but because of the location" — he glanced over at the row of hanging rings we had hung between the two trees in the backyard — "we'll have to do some hand digging. The tree roots will get damaged if I'm too aggressive with the excavator."

Mom sighed.

"I love digging!" Georgia threw her arms up in the air.

It didn't take Dad long to break ground and start moving bucket after bucket of dirt and grass. He soon hopped out of the cab and went into the garage. When he came back out, his arms were full of shovels and spades.

Initially, Dad held out a shovel for me, but quickly looked at my wrist and remembered I still needed to rest it.

Dad even gave Georgia a shovel. Sure, it was yellow plastic and made for beach sand, but still, I felt a bit useless being out here and not helping in any way.

Lydia drove the tip of her shovel into the ground and held it there. She asked, "So Evan, my younger brother. How will you contribute to this day?"

I had been wondering the same thing. "Maybe I could be site supervisor."

Dad's steely expression broke and he chuckled. He liked construction jokes. A lot.

"No, seriously, what are you going to *do*?" Lydia said. "We're all going to be out here getting sweaty and sore. You've got to do *something*."

I sat down on one of the log stumps and did a V-sit. It's a tough core workout. "I'll be your gofer. Gets drinks, sweat rags, stuff like that." I hopped off the log and saluted. "Butler Evan at your service."

Georgia started giggling. "Ehbun funny!"

"I'm getting sore just thinking about this," Mom complained. Using her shovel like a walking stick, Mom headed to a corner of the space Dad had already partially dug. With her foot against the top of edge of the blade, she drove the tip of the shovel into the ground.

"Go get everyone a drink," Lydia ordered as she plunged her shovel into the dirt. "We're going to need it!" She sent a pile of dirt flying.

At last, after Dad was satisfied that the bottom of the pit was even, and that the corners were square, the dig was done. My entire family was exhausted — Georgia had toddler fatigue; Mom, Dad, and Lydia ached everywhere from digging; and I was worn out from grueling butler duties. I lost count of how many times I had to go inside the house for various reasons.

"The pit would have been fine without the hand dig," Mom complained.

Dad glared at her. "It needed to be done properly for the liner to fit nicely."

I stepped in quickly. "You all did a great job. Thank

you." They all looked so wiped — nobody even responded to me.

We sat silent for a moment, staring at the rectangular hole. It was about six feet long, four feet wide, and two and a half feet deep. My family had done all this for a mud pit. My family had done all this for me.

"I never want to see another tree root." Lydia lay down on the ground.

I peered deep into the fresh hole in the ground. It was almost ready.

"Mom, did the liner arrive yet?" I asked. "Can you install it now?"

For some reason, this question made everybody mad. It was like the entire family was shooting eye daggers at me.

"No, it's not here yet," Mom snapped.

Georgia burst into tears. "Not funny! Where's funny Ehbun?" She rubbed her eyes furiously as tears streamed down her grimy face. They say playing in the dirt is good for a kid's immune system. Georgia was going to live to a hundred.

"Evan, will you take her upstairs?" Mom asked. She plopped herself down next to Lydia.

Georgia kept crying. "Not tired!" She swung her shoulders around in protest, fighting an imaginary sleep demon.

I got up from the lawn chair, which I had hoped to spend more time sitting on than I actually had, and hopped toward her like a frog. "Come on, kid, I'll give you a piggyback."

"No! No piggyback!" Georgia refused. She slapped the sleep monster away.

No piggyback? This was serious. My mind scrambled for an alternative.

Georgia wailed some more.

"How about I carry you like a *boulder over my shoulder*?" I suggested, raising my eyebrows.

She stopped crying.

"Funny Ehbun is back. Carry me." She lifted her arms and wriggled her fingers.

"Watch your wrist!" Mom warned.

I carefully picked up my little sister and slung her over my shoulder.

"You don't have to go to the bathroom, do you?" I asked as I started walking.

"I can hold it," Georgia replied.

It was the least comforting answer she could have given.

"Faster!" She slapped my back.

"How much do you weigh?" Seemed to me that the *Boulder over the Shoulder* thing wasn't too hard. I started to multitask and did lunges as I carried her through the house.

"I don't know! *Shhh*. Boulders don't talk." Georgia clamped her lips together and acted like a rock.

This was getting even better! I would have paid money for her to be quiet, but instead, all I had to do was to tell her she was a boulder! Why hadn't I thought of this before?

Carefully using mostly my left hand and only the crook of my right arm, I dropped her down onto her toddler bed.

Hovering above her, I took in the sight of my little sister. The word *disaster* came to mind immediately. Her clothes were absolutely disgusting. It seemed wrong to let her sleep like that, but Mom had not mentioned changing her clothes. Or washing her face. Or her hands. Or taking her to the washroom first.

I leaned over her and whispered, "Boulders sleep for a *long* time. Boulders are *very* silent."

She put a finger up to her lips and closed her eyes. Just like that, she let me *leave*. She didn't demand a story or anything! I felt like I had just won a lottery jackpot. I closed the door as quickly and as quietly as I could before I headed back downstairs.

Like silent, dirty zombies, the rest of my family had come back inside and were dragging themselves to the washrooms. Lydia went to the big washroom that the kids all shared, and Mom and Dad disappeared into their washroom. Nobody said a word.

For the first time all day, I could be alone outside. I dashed to the backyard and hopped into the hole my family had dug out.

We were still going to have to get it filled with mud after we installed the liner, but I just wanted to imagine how much fun this was going to be while we waited. Dad had a buddy who owed him a favor. He said that he'd be by later in the week with some clay and dirt and we'd just have to add water.

I closed my eyes and pretended I was powering my way through the mud patch. I could totally see it. This was going to be *my* event. Mostly leg strength, no wrists involved.

A big silly grin spread over my face. Had it been only a week ago when I was moping around having Sulking Time and feeling super sorry for myself? But now, so much had changed!

This Soiled Pants: Family Edition thing was turning out okay.

15

A JOG THAT WASN'T

"COME ON, TEAM PARK!" DAD CLAPPED HIS HANDS together after everybody had eaten some breakfast. Nobody had fully recovered from yesterday's big dig — except for Dad. He had put on shorts and a T-shirt. "Let's go out for a jog."

Mom and Lydia looked at him like he had misplaced his mind and it was nowhere to be found.

"What's that?" Georgia finally asked.

"It's a kind of running that is mostly unnecessary," Lydia told her.

"I love running!" Georgia said.

I didn't *love* running, but I knew it was a good cardio workout. "I'm in!" I told him.

Dad nodded his approval. "What about the rest of you?"

Lydia frowned and Mom refused to look at him in the eye.

"Come on! It's a beautiful Sunday. How about a run around Stanley Park?" Dad suggested.

Finally looking at him, Mom asked, "Which part?"

"Well, the whole park. Around the seawall. Once you start it, you've got to finish it."

"The *whole park*?" our entire family said at the same time. Except Georgia. She said, "I'm a whole Park too!"

Lydia typed furiously on her iPad. "The seawall is TWELVE kilometers!"

"I don't even think I can run twelve *meters* right now. I'm still aching from yesterday," Mom complained. "I can't do it." She waved both hands in the air to indicate her surrender.

She needed to get downstairs and ride that stationary bike more than I realized. I was going to have to find a way to motivate her more. But I did sort of agree that starting off with a twelve-kilometer run might be a bit extreme.

"We don't have much time to get ready for the big event! What is it, in like, five, six weeks?" Dad said. "Think of it like a boot camp."

"I don't want to go to boot camp." Lydia pouted. "I thought this was supposed to be *fun*."

"How about we start with a walk in the neighborhood?" Mom said. "If you want to run, you run. If you want to walk, you walk. Something *doable*."

"Fine, you all walk, I'll run with Ev." Dad started stretching. He twisted his torso a few times before he bent over and tried to touch his toes. I heard several joints crack.

He was strong, but not flexible.

I followed his lead and started to warm up. I was kind of excited. Dad and I had never been out on a jog together. We were training *together*, for real.

"What happened to me?" Dad gasped for air. "Geez, my knee is acting up again."

I hadn't even had time to worry about the butterflies I was feeling in my stomach over officially "training" with Dad, because as soon as we set foot on the sidewalk in front of the house, he had decided to take off at a sprint. I'd had a hard time keeping up with him, for about ten seconds. His pace then relaxed. After another half a block, the relaxed pace came to a complete standstill.

Dad was breathing heavily and his hunched posture might have been an early indicator of potential vomit, so I made sure to give him plenty of space.

Mom, Lydia, and Georgia caught up to us while Dad struggled to breathe.

"Back in high school, I used to run two kilometers as a warm-up *before* practice." Dad panted. He was still bent over with his hands on his knees.

Mom patted his back. "Then life happened. And that's *okay*. Don't kill yourself."

"Please don't throw up." Lydia grimaced at the thought.

Dad managed to lift his torso upright. "I guess the Seahawks don't start the preseason in tip-top shape either. Seems like it'll take a bit more work."

Our morning jog was over. I could have gone longer, but it turned out that my training partner had no cardio endurance. I mean, he was still strong and could lift or carry way more than I could, but I was surprised by what I saw. The wheezing he was doing was hard to ignore. All former high school rugby players get old, I guess.

"Carry me." Georgia pulled at Dad's hand.

"Hop up." He squatted to let Georgia jump on his back.

"Daddy's back is all wet!" She squeezed his neck tight.

"I was working hard!"

"Gross," Lydia mumbled to herself.

"We should still set a goal," Dad said. "How far should we walk?"

"I find I'm motivated by the thought of fresh croissants," Lydia said.

"To the bakery then," Mom said decidedly.

A walk to a bakery seemed to negate the benefits of the actual walk, but I had to admit, I enjoyed the local bakery's pain au chocolat. But this was the lowest-quality training I could imagine.

As I stared down at the squares of concrete that made up the sidewalk, I decided I could turn this simple walk into something else.

If I changed my stride, I could put one foot in each square while walking. Touching cracks between each square was against the rules too.

"What *are* you doing?" Lydia asked.

"The one-foot-per-square challenge. Normal walking is boring. This keeps me interested."

"Somehow, you look like a flamingo." Despite mocking me, Lydia tried it too.

Lydia didn't look exactly elegant as she stretched out her leg. There *was* something flamingo-y about it. But it was fun. It was impossible not to smile while doing the one-foot-per-square challenge.

Soon, we were all doing the flamingo walk. Everybody was laughing. An elderly woman holding a rake in her front yard stopped what she was doing and stared at us from across the street. She wasn't smiling. That's because she was just *watching* and not actually *doing* it. If she would only try it, she would eventually be smiling too.

"Georgia do!" She squirmed off Dad's back.

Her legs were awfully short, and there was no physical way she could do it. But she kept trying anyway.

After one final and fatally unsuccessful attempt, Georgia sat down on the sidewalk and cried.

"I can't do it!" she wailed. "Three-and-a-half is too little!" Then she started crawling on the front lawn of the house we had stopped in front of. "I'm just a baby!" Georgia was acting even more strangely than usual. "Babies are only good for crawling." She hauled herself around in jerky circles.

This display was weird, even by Georgia standards. It needed to stop. I stepped closer to her.

"You're not a baby!" I said in my best *I'm talking to a toddler* voice. I spoke with my whole face — exaggerated eyes, big mouth, and squeaky voice.

Georgia looked up at me from the ground. I had gotten her attention at least.

"You're a boulder," I said to her slowly, hoping my words would cause a hypnotic state.

Her face brightened and she put her index finger up to her lips. "*Shhh.*"

"That's right, boulders are very silent." I reached over and picked her up. The spell was working again! Georgia appeared to be in a trance.

"Watch your wrist," Mom said quietly and quickly.

I flung my sister over my shoulder. I knew how to do it without straining my right wrist.

"Like magic," Lydia whispered.

16

FOLLOW INSTRUCTIONS

THE LINER HAD ARRIVED YESTERDAY MORNING, and good thing too — it was hard to believe, but it was the last week of July already! Dad and I lined the hole with it after dinner yesterday, and it was a perfect fit. I had to admit, Dad was good with a measuring tape. We drove stakes into the corners so it wouldn't slip or move.

This morning, the distinctive beeping of a large construction vehicle backing up drew my attention. It was here! I ran to the window.

It wasn't just one large dump truck. There were *two*. They parked in front of the house with their lights flashing.

Mom scurried to find some shoes and went outside to talk to one of the drivers.

Then a third vehicle arrived with a flatbed trailer carrying a small excavator, similar to the one Dad had brought home on the weekend to dig the hole. The street was crowded with machinery. Even idling, the engine noises from all the trucks filled the house.

Lydia joined me at the window. "All this for a mud pit?" she asked.

I had been thinking the same thing. When Dad said the mud was coming today, I had imagined a driver would show up, throw a few bags of dirt in our front yard, and leave.

Mom gestured to the backyard to one of the drivers before heading back inside. This driver yelled instructions to the excavator operator, who started to drive slowly down the small ramp, off the trailer.

"Well, this is classic Dad overkill. But they'll be done pretty quick. It's just a few buckets," Mom said as she came back inside.

Georgia came to the window too. She pressed her nose to the glass. "Dump trucks dumping!"

The first dump truck raised its back bed, the tailgate lifted, and some sand came sliding out the back. It all landed on the road in front of the house.

Then the truck closed its tailgate and drove away. The second dump truck took its place and did the same thing, but this mix was different. Not sand. But not loose soil either. More like clay.

As soon as the second dump truck pulled away, the small excavator got to work. It picked up a bucket full of sand and then drove onto our grass and disappeared down the side of the house. We all ran to the back window.

It dumped the first bucket into the pit and then headed back for another load.

The driver kept alternating between the sand and the clay mix until the pile on the road in front of the house was gone and the pile in the pit was full. It was almost exactly right.

I had to concede that Dad was pretty good with a calculator.

"Okay, this is where we take over," Mom said. "Maybe get your bathing suits on or clothes that you don't mind ruining. This might be hot and messy." A small smile emerged, and she added, "But fun."

Dad had left clear, typed directions with Mom.

INSTRUCTIONS FOR A GOOD MUD MIX:

1. The pit should be overfilled slightly to account for settling. Make sure the drivers do it right.
2. Approximately 10 liters of water per square meter, got it? Adjust accordingly, based on viscosity.
3. The pit is **LINED**, which is great for keeping the mud stable. It must not be **OVERFILLED**, okay? Seems to contradict #1, but trust me, it doesn't.

4. Mix at regular intervals (use long-handled shovel – sorry, only one, others can use a piece of lumber. I cut into a manageable thickness for you and added a paddle on the bottom).

5. Keep the mud in the pit.

Lydia and I read the instructions with Mom.

"How do we make good mud?" Georgia asked eagerly while waiting for us to finish reading.

Mom folded the paper and tossed it in the recycling box. "You add water."

After we changed and we all moved outside, I noted that Mom had *not* put on her bathing suit or even changed her clothes at all.

Mom went to the side of the house and passed Lydia a hose. "Take this. Walk it closer to the pit."

Then she walked over to the other side of the house where there was another outdoor tap and passed me a second hose. "Follow your sister."

"Where's *my* hose?" Georgia asked.

"You're a tiny bit too young to have your own hose. But I'm sure your brother and sister will let you help with theirs."

Georgia was very dissatisfied. Her crossed arms and the giant pout on her face let everybody know exactly how she felt.

Mom looked around the backyard. She passed Georgia a watering can.

"It's empty!" Georgia complained.

By now, I could tell when Georgia was going to start acting like a weirdo. I quickly intervened.

"No, it's not *empty*." I was testing my mind-bending powers again. "You just have very, very light water. So light, you can't even *see* it."

"Light water!" Lydia exclaimed, overacting, but not enough for a toddler to notice. "That's *very* special. Why is light water only for three-and-a-half-year-olds?"

Georgia beamed. She stared deeply into her empty watering can. Happily, she took it carefully to the edge of the soon-to-be mud pit.

Mom looked fondly at us. "I'm so proud of you two."

"Because we're a bunch of fakes?" I whispered as I watched Georgia tipping the watering can over the mud pit.

"No, because you're taking care of each other." Mom squeezed my good arm. "Speaking of taking care of each other . . . " she continued. "I'm going to practice self-care. I think I might use this time to ride my bike while you two handle everything."

"The *bike*?" I asked, pointing in the general direction of the basement.

Lydia and I looked at each other, surprised, but also happy with her initiative. That was *great* news. I had been wondering how to get her on that thing. Maybe all this excitement about getting ready for the Soiled Pants race was finally starting to rub off.

"Yeah, the laundry rack with wheels." Mom smiled. "Don't make me self-conscious. But watching your dad try to jog reminded me that I used to cycle to UBC when I was a student, and I didn't even vomit most days. There's that really big hill on 16th Avenue too. I used to be able to climb it without getting off my bike and walking."

"That's really great, Mom! But what about Dad's instructions? How will we know if we're doing it right?" Lydia asked. "You're sure you're okay leaving us?"

Mom scoffed. "It's a *mud pit.* Why'd he have to get all project manager-y on us? Just fill it with water. Stop when it looks like mud. How hard can it be?"

"Quit it!" Lydia screamed at me.

She was currently in that strange emotional zone where she was annoyed but also laughing hysterically. It was as if she kept switching between rage and giggles every two seconds. It made me confused, so I kept spraying her, stopping, and then starting again. I thought of it like preparing for the finale of Soiled Pants where I'd be able to spray her freely.

We had been left unsupervised with two water hoses,

an empty but magical watering can, and a freshly filled pit that was turning into a nice soupy mix of soft, squishy mud. There was only one inevitable outcome to this scenario — a giant mess.

Among the water, the mud, and no parental boundaries, Lydia, Georgia, and I laughed and screamed for a long time.

But then the project manager came home.

"What's going on here?" Dad's voice boomed across the backyard.

We froze. He had snuck up on us. He usually parked the truck in the garage at the back of the house where we would have had some notice of his arrival, but today he must have parked out front.

I stopped squeezing the trigger on the hose, and the backyard was suddenly very quiet.

Dad approached us slowly. His eyes were wide open, as was his mouth.

He scanned the yard, from left to right. He scanned us, up and down.

I gulped. Dad looked really angry. He looked angry at *us*.

His eyes narrowed. His nostrils flared. His chest heaved.

"Look Daddy, magic light water!" Georgia broke the silence. He ignored her and the watering can she held up.

"Where is your mother?" His voice was quiet but had a sharp edge to it.

I nervously met his gaze. "Inside."

Dad turned on his heel and strode into the house.

We said nothing until Dad was inside.

"I don't think we measured the way he wanted," Lydia said in a hushed voice.

I looked behind us and stared at the yard.

It *was* a bit of a mess. *We* were a bit of a mess. But so what? It was supposed to be the Summer of Fun! How could we train for an event called Soiled Pants without getting a *little* dirty?

Lydia crept toward the house, leaning her right ear close to the back window.

"Ehbun, what's happening?" Georgia asked.

Lydia shushed her and continued to listen.

I squatted down to look at my little sister. "Can you use your magic water and start to clean up a little bit? I'm going to talk to Lydia."

Georgia nodded.

I inched carefully to where Lydia was standing, next to the window, out of sight.

There were loud voices inside the house.

"I left clear instructions!" Dad said. "Do I have to do everything myself to make sure it's done right?"

"Honestly, it's just a mud pit! Why do you have to be *such* a perfectionist? It's for the kids. My god, what *is* the big deal? You and your lists. You're driving us all crazy."

I got a funny feeling in my stomach. Then something slammed down hard. The sound of it shocked me and Lydia, and we both jumped.

Lydia cowered and covered her ears.

"Come on, we'd better clean up." I pulled Lydia's arm. I'd heard enough. The knots in my stomach felt like rocks, and I knew I couldn't hear anymore. "Let's stop listening."

Lydia looked down at the ground and nodded.

I pressed my lips together. I should have known from the look on Dad's face and from the way Mom had just thrown his list away that they were bound to end up like this.

"I wish we hadn't started this," I said as Lydia and I walked back to the mud pit. "This is sort of all my fault. They wouldn't be fighting if I was just playing video games by myself all day."

"You don't get it, do you? Mom and Dad fighting isn't your fault." She made sure I looked her in the eye. I knew she was right, but still, a hard nugget of guilt pressed against my chest and didn't want to move. "It's not our fault they sometimes forget how to be nice to each other." Lydia paused briefly. "And us."

I glanced at Georgia sitting in the backyard stirring the mud with a stick and lowered my voice. "Why can't adults be more *adult-y*? Why can't they *talk*? Nicely! Like anybody wants to listen to you when you're yelling."

"Exactly," Lydia agreed. She picked up a hose. "We'd better clean up. Let's spray the grass clean, at least."

As I tried to wash the dirt away from places it wasn't supposed to be, I couldn't help but wonder — how was Team Park going to be successful in a Soiled Pants competition when we couldn't even agree on the best way to make mud?

17

A WALL CAN BE BUILT IN ONE DAY

NOW THAT THE OBSTACLE WITH THE HANGING rings and the mud pit below was complete, the backyard was starting to look like a proper Soiled Pants race. It was hard to enjoy it yesterday, because of what went on between my parents. But today was a new day. My wrist was better too. It had been two weeks since I had reinjured it. It was time to get back out there and see what I could do. But I was nervous about it. The last thing I wanted was to hurt myself *again*.

I snapped a picture for Davey and Aaron. With it, a simple message:

MUD pit!

I waited a few seconds for a reply, but neither of them

responded. What time was it in China anyway? Maybe Davey was sleeping. Maybe Aaron was paddling or out picking berries. I shrugged and put down the iPad. There was no point in waiting for a reply — instead, I should *do* something with my day.

After having it for over a month, the trampoline had lost some of its initial luster, and even Lydia didn't jump on it regularly anymore. Shiny new toys get dull pretty fast. Lydia and Georgia wouldn't bother me outside today. I'd be able to practice alone.

The old Evan, the Dominator Ninja Evan, liked alone. The Soiled Pants Evan realized that alone was lonely. We were supposed to be doing this *together*. Even though Mom and Dad weren't giving each other the silent treatment today, we hardly felt like a unified team. This was a problem.

We were losing momentum. I could feel it. The race was soon — only four and a half weeks! — but just a little too far away for us to be really concerned about it. But we really should have been! Aside from Lydia, were any of us even remotely close to being able to actually do the course well? I was really starting to have my doubts. We were going to have to kick it into high gear, or we were going to get our butts kicked.

I needed to hop into that mud pit and give it everything I had.

The back door opened and Georgia waddled outside with Lydia trailing behind her. Georgia gripped the spindles of the railing on her way down the back stairs.

"Ehbun training?" Georgia asked.

"I'm thinking about it." I scanned the backyard with my hands on my hips. "What's everybody else doing?"

"Mommy turning pain into power."

"Huh?"

"Mommy go Peloton." Georgia raised a fist to the sky.

"She's on the bike again. Can you believe it?" Lydia asked.

"Wow!" I exclaimed. Mom was doing it. She was trying her best. I kind of felt proud of her right now — the middle-aged mom that wouldn't quit. "But you know it's not even a real Peloton, right? Who can afford that? It's a knockoff from Canadian Tire."

Georgia pretended to hunch over a pair of invisible handlebars. "So what? Ride to give it! Ride to live it!"

"We watched Mom ride the bike while the video coach was on for a minute until she told us to get lost," Lydia said, explaining Georgia's strange outburst.

"That ain't pain! That's just the fear trying to hold you down!" Georgia continued.

"At least Mom's having fun," I said.

"No, Mommy not having fun. Her face looks angry. But Mommy trying anyway," Georgia said. "Maybe the fun will come later."

Georgia was almost four, and most of the time what she said was weird or ridiculous, but this time, I sure hoped that she was right.

After rummaging through my drawers, I put on a grungy shirt and an old pair of shorts that I had found. These clothes would be ruined, and I was okay with that. They would be my official training-in-mud clothes. Before I headed back outside, I got a glass of water. While I drank, I stared at the Summer of Fun poster on the refrigerator as a reminder to myself. Why was having fun turning into so much work? *The fun will come later*, I told myself.

For just a second, I thought about Darren. I was sure he was training his heart out to do his absolute best for the Dominator Ninja in Seattle. I didn't want to go back to physio sessions, but I did miss his energy and passion. I tried to channel some of it.

All the way from the basement, I could hear the video coach shouting encouraging things to Mom on her bike. It was funny because this video coach wasn't like Darren at all. They had an aggressive *You'd better do this, and you'd better do this NOW* attitude. Darren would always say things firmly but gently. He never let me quit. Darren really was an excellent physiotherapist. I hoped he was going to make it to the top of Pinnacle Peak and feel the confetti sprinkling down around him. I wasn't going to get any confetti, not this year anyway, but I wanted to feel a little sense of satisfaction sprinkling down on me too. So, I'd better get to work.

After hopping down into the mud, my immediate reaction was a shudder — it felt squishy and cold. The plastic liner at the very bottom of the pit made me think that I was going to slip at any time, but I managed to get used to the feel of it. In mud up to my thighs, even walking was hard. But that's what I did, over and over, back and forth until my legs burned.

Without practice, how could there be success? Maybe trudging through mud wasn't exactly the most skilled event at Soiled Pants, but it was an event that needed to be completed, so I was going to do my best to become the best mud walker I could be.

When I finally got tired of the mud, I went to the hose and washed myself off. There was nothing like a burst of cold water to revitalize the soul.

Lydia and Georgia came into the yard while I was still standing by the side of the house with the hose.

"Lydia?" I called out to her.

Lydia grabbed the first ring and scampered across the whole row. She made it look as easy as walking. "Yeah?" She avoided the mud pit and landed on the grass.

"We need to practice. Together."

She tilted her head.

"I just think we need better teamwork," I said.

"I don't disagree with you. But with Dad at work most of the time, it's hard. Anyway, there's only one event we all need to finish."

Storm the Wall.

"How can we practice that anyway?" Lydia asked.

It *was* a problem.

The next day at breakfast, Dad should have been getting ready to go to work, but instead, he was hunched over a large piece of paper.

"Good morning," I said, rubbing my eyes.

"You're up early. Mom's not even awake yet."

"Yeah, I realized there's not much time to practice. I thought I'd go for a jog or something."

"I like your attitude!" Dad said. He sipped his coffee. "I'm sorry I haven't been the best training partner. Work has been busy. But I think you'll like *this*." He tapped the paper.

"What is it?" I pulled up a chair.

"I'm going to build a wall."

"Oh, really! That's exactly what we need!" It was as if Dad had read my mind. I couldn't remember when we had been on the same page like this before. "When did you draw this?"

"Last night. I thought it would be good to practice the *Storm the Wall* portion before the event, don't you think?" Dad asked.

"I had been thinking the same thing!"

"Now, I don't have the *exact* dimensions, but I emailed the organizers last night to ask for them . . ." Dad checked his phone. "No, they didn't reply yet. I mean, I have a pretty good idea of approximately how tall it is, but I don't want to get it wrong. It seems like for the family events, the walls are usually shorter, but I don't know exactly. Being off by a few inches could be disastrous."

I considered it all for a minute. Measuring a skyscraper wrong was disastrous. Miscalculating measurements for a wooden wall for an event that involved mostly mud just seemed like a *whoops* kind of mistake.

"Let's watch one more video, so I have a good sense of exactly what I need to build. If one of the carpenters on-site has time today, I'm going to ask them to help whip up a frame."

I moved my chair closer to Dad as he opened a YouTube video. "Darn ads." He tapped his fingers impatiently while we waited for the ad to play.

"*Opening soon! Vancouver's Agile Ninja Training Centre! The best local training ground. State-of-the-art ninja equipment . . .*"

Dad's finger hovered over the "skip ad" button.

"Wait!" I put my hand on his to stop him. The video showed the interior. I could not keep my mouth closed. It was awesome. Incredible. It was huge. Rings. Salmon ladders. Three sizes of warped walls. A peg wall. A climbing wall. Bars and nets everywhere. People standing around, training, and laughing together. One particular person made me do a double take. Darren! Had that been Darren? It sure looked like him. I held back a laugh. It wouldn't surprise me one bit if he was already a member.

"*Sign up today. Memberships are almost sold out! Unlock your inner ninja!*"

"Agile Ninja Training Centre!" I practically yelled. "That's the place they're giving away a free family membership for at the Soiled Pants race!"

"Looks pretty posh in there. The memberships are probably expensive," Dad said. "All that high-end equipment!"

I nodded. It *did* seem kind of fancy — next-level even. It had sounded awesome, but now that I had *seen* what it was like with my own eyes, it was even more amazing than I could have imagined! I would have given anything to get a chance to train there.

Dad typed on his phone.

"Two thousand dollars a year! That's outrageous! Look!" He showed me the screen with the prices. "That's for *one* person!"

Ouch. That *was* pricey. Next-level is expensive. "They do provide individualized training, it says."

"We're building a perfectly fine obstacle course in our backyard for almost nothing!" He shook his head and muttered. "Two thousand dollars a year . . ."

I pressed my lips together.

"I'll build you a good wall in the backyard. You don't need a fancy gym like that." Dad glanced at his watch. "Oh, geez. It's late. Gotta go."

He quickly rolled up the paper with the drawing for the wall and headed to work.

After Dad left, I went to the Soiled Pants race site. I checked out the information one more time: *All participants who finish the race will receive a chance to win a one-year free family membership to the all-new Agile Ninja Training Centre.*

It wasn't like I had a secret stash of cash under my mattress. I wasn't going to be able to pay for it on my own, and Dad had made it pretty clear how he felt about buying a membership. But there was still a shot we could *win* a free membership. We could afford free. We just needed to make sure we finished the course to have our shot.

Dad couldn't build that wall fast enough.

18

GOOD COMMUNICATION

"EV, I NEED YOUR HELP." DAD POKED HIS HEAD
inside the back door when he got home that night.

"Wall stuff?" I asked, sitting up. I'd been waiting for
him all day.

"I can help too," Lydia said.

Dad looked uncertain. "Sure, I guess."

"Why'd you say it like *that*?" Lydia asked.

"It's just there's some heavy lifting." He quickly turned
and headed back to the garage before Lydia could answer.

"Ugh. I *hate* it when he makes gender-based *assump-
tions* about me." Lydia stomped outside.

"Ev, your wrist is good?" Mom asked as I slipped into
sandals.

"Yeah, pretty good."

"Be careful."

"Yup."

Dad's truck was jammed full of pieces of wood.

"Luckily, one of the carpenters at the job site was able to make this really quick for me today," Dad told us. "It's in a few parts, so I could bring it home. We'll have to put it together in the backyard."

"Did they email you back with the exact dimensions?" I asked.

"No, I got tired of waiting. I sent a nudge email too, but nothing. I just used my best guess based on some research. We made it twelve feet high." Dad unhooked a nylon strap that had secured the wall on the drive home. "It usually looks like the same simple wall in all the event pictures and videos. Although, once in a while, they add something unusual. But not often. You hold on to the end."

I braced myself for the wooden structure that was coming my way. I almost fumbled it.

"Geez! Don't drop it, Ev!" Dad shouted. Lydia swooped in next to me to help.

"Thanks," I murmured to her.

"I know I'm just a girl, but once in a while, I *can* come in handy," she hissed.

I don't know why she was so mad at *me*. *I* never assumed she couldn't do anything because she was a girl. That was Dad!

"Don't spit your fire at *me*," I whispered.

"He has thick, oblivious skin," she whispered back. "Sorry, unfairly blaming you for all your gender's wrongs."

"Got a firm hold? Make sure you do!" Dad hopped down from the truck. "Back up slowly."

Between the three of us, we carried three more pieces off the cargo bed. It had been hard to envision while they were strapped to the truck, but now, with the wood on the ground, I could see it. An imposing wall of plywood, with support brackets to hold it in place.

I could hardly believe it. Right here in the backyard was our own personal wall obstacle. The backyard looked almost like a proper Soiled Pants course now!

The plywood surface was smooth, and with no hand holds or places to grip, it was definitely going to be difficult to get over, but not impossible.

Dad drove in the final screw and stepped back.

"Thanks, Dad. This is going to be fun."

"Come in! Dinner's ready," Mom said from the back door. "Gosh, that thing is tall . . ."

"Do we have time to practice it — all together?" I asked her.

"Uh, why don't you eat dinner first. Looks like we'll need some energy."

"We'll practice later. Get really good at it." Dad put down his tool belt.

"Got it." Nobody was going to practice harder than me.

I needed to do something about our weakest links. For the last two days, Mom had been putting off our group wall practice. Even though she had surprised me a couple of times by riding the stationary bike, it wasn't enough. It always seemed that she was busy with other things.

As a result, I was going to do something out of character. Something I never thought in a million years I'd *willingly* volunteer to do — babysit Georgia.

"Mom?" I was even helping her tidy up after breakfast.

"Hmm?" She tucked plates into the dishwasher.

"Do you need a break today? Some *personal* time?" I asked.

"That sounds good." Then her eyebrows creased. "Why?"

"Remember how you said you used to ride your bike up a really big hill when you were in university? Remember? Well, I was watching this YouTube vlog about a guy who bought a stationary bike. He was chronicling his experience with it. He rode it every day for two weeks for thirty minutes each day. Did you know that before he started his experiment he had very poor lung capacity? Like below average. After his two weeks, he went to ninety-fifth percentile for his age. Pretty impressive, huh?"

Her eyes narrowed. "Sure. If you've got nothing but time."

"I'm going to give you some of that rare personal time, right now! I'll babysit Georgia! You could get back on that bike!"

"What if I don't care about increasing my lung capacity?"

"Oh, it's not about increasing lung capacity. Not really." My mother's squint was growing more suspicious. I decided to try another angle. "He also felt *great*, like he let go of all of his daily stressors." I realized I may have sounded too enthusiastic. I reined it in a little. "The vlogger, I mean. He said it was challenging and everything, but that at the end, he felt super satisfied with himself."

In addition to squinting, Mom now had pursed lips.

"I mean, taking care of Georgia at your age must be stressful," I said.

Now instead of looking wary and doubtful, she looked irritated.

I should have just left convincing Mom to exercise more with Lydia. I wasn't doing a very good job.

"I mean, um . . ." I was floundering. Badly.

Lydia, piggybacking Georgia, came into the kitchen and pushed me aside. "I mean, you could do something else, but riding the bike will help you feel good. Whatever you decide, how about we just get out of your hair so you can have the house to yourself."

Mom resumed squinting. This time, at both of us. "Really? I'm allowed to take time for myself?"

"You deserve it," Lydia said.

Mom's gaze remained unconvinced.

"With the children away, a mother may play." Lydia smiled broadly.

Not to be outdone by Lydia's spontaneous catch-phrase, a cute little jingle came to my mind too. Before I could stop myself, I said, "A mom that's merry is a little less scary."

Lydia immediately pinched the back of my left arm.

"Ow!" I gave the spot a good rub. I should have tried harder to keep quiet.

"Not funny," Georgia said sternly.

"We'll be outside," Lydia said smoothly as she yanked me out of the kitchen. She hissed through gritted teeth, "Did you have to bring up her age *and* call her scary all in the same conversation?"

"Mommy is old and sometimes grouchy!" Georgia proclaimed softly, matching Lydia's hushed tone.

"Ugh." Lydia rolled her eyes. "How come the only one you can convince to do anything is Georgia?"

"I must have the mind of a toddler," I replied.

"Me too!" Georgia agreed.

"I bow to your interpersonal skills." I actually bowed to Lydia.

Georgia, with her chin on Lydia's shoulder, giggled. "Ehbun funny again."

Lydia sighed heavily. "It's *such* a burden. Am I the only one in this whole house who knows how to communicate effectively?"

"Look around . . ." I said.

"Just try to watch and learn, okay? Maybe one day you can take over being the responsible one and let *me* be the teenager with raging hormones and a complete lack of self-awareness."

I smiled. "I'll try my best."

"Hurry up!" Georgia scolded. "Too much talking. Not enough *doing.*"

19

PERSONAL GROUP TIME

"OKAY, WE'VE GOT TO GET SERIOUS ABOUT THIS,"
I said as we vacated the house and left Mom alone.

Lydia was headed to the trampoline, but I wanted to talk about strategy. I hoped Mom was using this time efficiently. And by *efficiently*, I meant I hoped she was cycling her heart out.

"*Serious*? I don't know about *that*." Lydia did a small U-turn and joined me on a stump.

"Yes, serious! We need to win!"

I must have said something wrong, because Lydia dropped her head to the left and her eyes expanded into enraged discs. "Do you hear yourself?"

"What?"

"You sound exactly like *Dad*."

I twisted my mouth. Do I?

"I'm not like Dad at all," I mumbled.

"The Summer of Fun. Remember? You wanted to have *fun*. Just don't forget that, okay?"

"I haven't forgotten!" I bristled. I was still annoyed and confused with the comparison to Dad.

"I understand that maybe a competition, to some, is all about winning. I totally get that."

"Winning is not everything!" Georgia shouted. She had been filling a bucket with mud from the pit. "Second-best book says so!"

"Exactly. I never go to a gymnastics competition thinking about the podium. I go because I want to show *myself* what I can do. There's a sweet spot you have to find between being competitive and doing your best, all while not being a jerk at the same time."

I stared at my sister. She knew more about this kind of thing than I did. *Find the sweet spot.*

"I'm not saying it's *easy*." Lydia stopped looking annoyed with me. "But you've also got to get real. We've never done a Soiled Pants race before. I bet a lot of other people who have entered *have*. We're not experienced."

"Then we've got to make up for it with enthusiasm! And determination!"

Lydia seemed less tense now. "All right. I've got to respect the passion."

I thought about what Lydia was saying. "Let me say it

differently. I don't *need* to win, but I would very much like to try my absolute best to do everything I can so we have a *shot* at winning."

Lydia raised her eyebrows. "Just don't forget the sweet spot, okay?"

"Okay. But we *do* need a game plan."

"Let me guess. You've already given it some thought."

I smiled. Of course I had. On the pad of paper I had brought outside, I drew a small chart.

"So, if I remember correctly, these are the events, right?" I showed Lydia my list.

"I think so."

"So, let's assign events. And figure out what each person has to do to practice for that event."

"This is turning into homework." Lydia rolled her eyes.

After some discussion, Lydia and I decided:

EVENT	PERSON	TRAINING NEEDED
Mucky Mud Pit	Evan	More practice. Get dirty.
Clunky Monkey Bars	Lydia	None.
Boulder over the Shoulder	Dad	Find rice sack. Move it aimlessly.
Sticky Spiderweb Net	Georgia ??	More playground time.
Dodge the Log	Mom ????	???? Too much to list.
Storm the Wall	Team Park	Team practice? When???

"What will Georgia do?" Georgia asked.

"You'll rock it on the *Sticky Spiderweb!*" I told her. "You can climb all those rope ladders at the playground, right?"

"Right! I love sticky things!" Georgia smashed mud in between her fingers.

"Mom," I said. "How can she train for *Dodge the Log*?"

Lydia paused before she replied. "During the videos, it seems like there is a lot of ducking. To avoid the swinging logs. A lot of squats? Lunges?"

"*You* tell her."

"Georgia do it!" She raised her hand.

I laughed. "Sure, let's see how she takes it."

"I always tell her what to do. She does it," Georgia said.

"Toddler power!" Lydia gave Georgia a high five.

"Okay, back to training. Wanna try to scale the wall?" I asked. "Together?"

"Just the three of us?" Lydia asked. She glanced at Georgia.

"We could ask Mom to join us," I suggested. "But every time I've asked, she's been busy."

"Didn't we *just* tell her she could have personal time?" Lydia asked.

"We didn't say how *much* time . . ."

"Georgia do!" This time, she got up and waddled inside as quickly as her short legs would take her.

Lydia did a few rounds on the hanging rings while we waited for Georgia to possibly come back with Mom.

I stood under the wall. Even if I jumped as high as I could, the tips of my fingers didn't come close to reaching the top. I could see why this was always the final event. You really needed a group of people to make it work. You needed teamwork.

When the back door opened, I could see that Mom *had* been on the bike. Her cheeks were flushed and pieces of her hair were stuck to her forehead. Good signs that she had worked up a nice sweat.

"Hurry, Mommy." Georgia pulled at Mom's hand.

"Now? We have to do this now?" she asked. "What about my personal time?"

"If it don't burn, how will you learn?" Georgia shouted.

"It's fun, right?" Mom asked doubtfully.

I glanced at Lydia instead of answering.

"Mom, I can't promise it's going to be fun right away. But we're going to try to make it fun by the end." Lydia smiled sweetly at Mom. I scribbled down notes mentally.

She looked uneasy, but said, "Okay, I'm already a bit of a mess. I guess we can't put it off any longer. Let's try."

The four of us stood in front of the wall. Mom put her hands on her hips. "Well, any ideas?" she asked me.

"There's the classic, most basic way to get over — using your team members' hands as a step." I laced my fingers and held my palms up.

"I'm not stepping on your hands," Mom said.

I had forgotten about my wrist for just a minute. Probably wouldn't be too smart to test it with Mom's full weight. Not right now, anyway. "Oh, right. You could use my thigh instead." I squatted into position to show her.

"Okay, that seems like it could work. Is there any reason you want me to go first?" she asked while she contemplated the wall.

"Because you're . . ."

Lydia cut off the rest of my thought. The word *old* was just on the tip of my tongue. "We think it's the best strategy," Lydia said loudly, followed by a very focused glare at me.

"Okay, shall we?" Mom looked as ready as she could be.

I stood with my right shoulder to the wall and my right leg bent at the knee. My left leg was extended behind and locked into position, acting like an anchor.

Lydia did the same thing but in reverse, so that the two of us were staring at each other.

Mom kicked off her slippers and tentatively put her foot on my thigh.

She kept one foot on the ground and reached out to put her left hand on Lydia's shoulder for balance. Then she tried to push her weight up and reach for the top of the wall. The arch of her foot rocked back and forth over my thigh, and with her arms flailing in the air, she tumbled to the ground.

"Did it burn?" Georgia asked, standing over our fallen mother.

"It burns like crazy!" Mom grabbed her backside. But she was laughing. "I'm going to need more personal time now."

20

TEAM TIME

WHEN WE TOLD DAD THAT NIGHT WE HAD
practiced *Storm the Wall*, he looked very satisfied. But
then we also mentioned the potential problem we hadn't
seen until we were actually trying to do it.

Once we got *over* the wall, then what? It was a long way
down. It was built to a family-friendly height of twelve feet.
I found on a blog that the wall for the adult competition was
usually fifteen feet high. But still, twelve feet is pretty high.

We needed a place to land. In the Soiled Pants race,
I remembered seeing a raised platform on the back side
of the wall.

Problem: We didn't have a platform. Even with a garage
full of wood, it was going to be tough for Dad to just whip
one up.

We all stood around, staring at the wall, trying to find a solution.

Finally, Mom shouted, "The trampoline!"

I would like to say she didn't gloat, but she did. I pursed my lips as I thought it all through. The trampoline would give us a good place to land, that was for sure, but I realized that it didn't help with the second purpose of the platform — a place to stand to help other team members climb up. I shrugged. It was the best we could do for now.

"And *you* said it was a bad idea," Mom said mockingly to Dad. The smug look on her face wasn't helping. She could benefit from a quick tutorial on communication from Lydia too.

Dad stiffened. "You got lucky, Grace, that's all." He turned away from her. No doubt about it: he also needed to sign up for Lydia's class.

But luckily, it ended there, and instead of anything else strained between them, Dad got busy.

"Ev! Lydia! Grab the other end!" Dad started to drag the wall closer to the trampoline while Lydia and I pushed.

"Okay! Let's see how this will work!" Dad seemed satisfied with the new location. The top of the trampoline netting was just below the top of the wall, so we didn't even need to remove it. We were *finally* ready to practice climbing the wall. All of us.

"Climb up, Ev," Dad said. He stood solid and steady with his back against the wall, his feet digging into the ground. Dad didn't even mind when I basically kicked him in the cheek climbing on top of him.

Once I was steady on top of his shoulders, I wasn't sure my wrist was quite ready, but *I* was sure ready. I made a grab for the wall, and with Dad still giving me some support from underneath, I managed to clamber to the top!

"I did it!" Clinging with my chest pressed along the top of the wall, my right arm could almost touch the trampoline netting on the other side.

Mom and Lydia stood below. "Fling yourself over!" Lydia shouted.

When I hurled myself onto the middle of the trampoline, I bounced a few times on my feet before I collapsed onto my back. I stared up at the blue sky and realized that *this* was exactly what I wanted: the feeling of success.

I had Team Park on the right track. Sunday morning, Dad literally used a sack of rice to practice *Boulder over the Shoulder*. The big, huge one from Costco. That thing was fifty pounds!

While I waded in mud, Dad dashed around the backyard, weaving in and around the stumps with the sack of rice flung over his shoulder like it was a dish towel.

"That has got to be the most Asian training method *ever*," Lydia said from the trampoline. "If he starts carrying an earthenware pot full of kimchi, I'm going to make a meme."

Georgia came outside with Mom. Mom was carrying a small basket full of toys. The basket of toys was a bit weird. I wasn't sure why Georgia needed those outside; there was already plenty to do.

As soon as Mom placed the basket on the grass, Georgia immediately proceeded to dump its contents.

Mom sat down on a chair, but Georgia had other ideas. Georgia began to throw toys at Mom. They were mostly soft. Mostly.

"Hey!" Mom said. "What are you doing? You said you wanted to play with those!"

"Dodge this!" Georgia yelled.

I held back a laugh. Georgia was doing a very good job at getting Mom to do things that Mom wouldn't have willingly done otherwise. She had a different style than Lydia, but in the end, they both seemed to get things done.

"Don't throw things at me," Mom said in her best stern voice.

"Not throwing. You're practicing."

"How is this related to Soiled Pants training?" Mom asked. "Picking up toys seems more like a chore."

"Don't call it a 'chore.' You get the wrong mindset from the beginning. Call it Leg Day," I called from the mud pit.

"Ehbun funny." Georgia chuckled as she kicked toys farther away from one another.

I climbed out of the pit to show Mom. "You know, in *Dodge the Log*, you have to do a lot of squatting. Like this." I demonstrated. "A lot of quick, low movements. A real thigh burner."

"Again, I ask, how is picking up toys related?"

"Think about what you have to do to pick them up."

She picked up one toy slowly before putting it in the basket.

"Okay, so I'm bending and ducking."

"Quack, quack!" Georgia said as she reached into the basket to retrieve the toy Mom had just picked up. She threw it toward the garage.

Mom was defeated by our outstanding logic and gave in. She turned to Georgia. "Okay, let's see who can pick up the most toys the fastest!"

She chased, and Georgia started laughing as they sprinted to pick up toys.

"You're getting better at persuasion," Lydia whispered. "I am a very good role model."

I jumped. The last time I had noticed her, she had been on the trampoline. "Can you quit creeping up on me?"

"I can't help it, I'm light on my feet."

"Can you put that skill to some other use besides scaring me?"

"Not sure what else it's good for," Lydia replied.

"I'm sure you'll think of something."

21

START TO FINISH

NOW THAT WE HAD A WALL TO CLIMB AND A PLACE to land, we needed to do a practice race from start to finish, but Dad had to work, and after dinner, Mom never had any energy. So we could only do group practice on weekends. The first two weeks of August had passed in the blink of an eye, and I knew it was important we do a practice race, a whole race, before the actual event in three weeks.

Since it was Saturday, and we were finally all home together, we needed to practice *today*. Before the others joined me, I tried to plan out a backyard series of events that would be a close approximation of the real thing.

Five of the six obstacles were no problem. We had a mud pit. Check! We didn't have monkey bars, but the rings were close enough. Check! Dad was a master at Rice Sack over the Shoulder. Check! Mom had been picking up stuff for the last couple weeks thanks to Georgia. Her thighs must be like rocks by now. Check! The *Sticky Spiderweb Net* and Georgia were a big problem. I knew she could climb; I'd seen her do it at the Rideau Adventure Playground. But we didn't have anything to climb like that in the backyard. We'd have to do a substitution for her. I wasn't happy about it, but we didn't have a lot of options.

And after practicing it all of last weekend, we knew we could easily get one or two of us over the wall. We still couldn't practice getting all of us over it one after another — still no platform — but we all felt confident we'd manage during the real thing. I wasn't worried about that event at all.

"How's this going to work?" Lydia asked. She pulled out a packet of gum from her hoodie pocket, popped a square out, and placed it into her mouth. I heard the outer shell of the gum crack.

I stuck my hand out and she gave me a piece. "We can pretty much duplicate each event, except for Georgia's."

"Good thing she's flexible."

"Look!" Georgia stood in the doorway and bent her head to touch her knees. "Very flexible!"

Mom and Dad joined us outside. Dad carried the rice sack to the center of the yard and plunked it down on the grass. I was impressed by the sack's durability. Dad had put it through a lot. Based on the rough and dirty state of the bag's exterior, I was pretty sure we should never eat what was inside for dinner.

Mom tied up her hair into a short ponytail. "Okay, I'm as ready as I'll ever be." She put on her game face.

Dad, who pretty much *always* had a game face on, slapped his hands together. "Okay! Let's do this!"

Having the right mindset turned something that could have been tedious into something fun. We were all out here "training," but we were all also enjoying ourselves. It was the best of both worlds! Just another few practices and we'd be ready. Good thing too, because that's all the time we had.

"Okay, I'm going to start in the mud. Once I power through, I'll tag Lydia. Lydia will fly across the rings — let's just pretend they're monkey bars — and then she'll tag you, Dad. Dad, you carry the sack across the yard, I guess you could weave in and out of the stumps if you wanted, and then you tag Mom. Mom, pick up all that stuff on the ground and make sure you pretend that you're trying to avoid swinging logs. And then . . ."

I glanced down at my little sister.

"What Georgia do?" she yelled as she slapped her chest.

"Umm . . ."

"Hurry! Tell me!" She started hopping up and down frantically.

My mind raced. "This is a special event, okay?" I turned on my preschool teacher voice. "It's called . . . Burpsalot."

I ignored Lydia's incredulous stare.

"You do this ten times." I demonstrated a burpee. "And then you run to the wall and wait for us? Okay!" I turned up the enthusiasm dial to extremely high. I held out my hand for a high five.

Georgia slapped my hand with a surprising amount of force and yelled, "Okay!"

Dad pulled out his phone. "We should time ourselves, don't you think? Set a baseline for the next time we do it, and then we try to improve our times?"

Mom rolled her eyes. "It's not a competition."

"Actually, Mom, it *is*," Lydia said. "I think it's important to respect everybody's individual opinions and not be so quick to dismiss somebody's idea. I've learned in school that clearly expressing yourself in a nonjudgmental forum is the only way to work effectively as a group. We're Team Park, aren't we?"

"Yes," Mom answered reluctantly.

"Sometimes you need to trust the opinions of your teammates. Don't you think? Mom? Dad?"

They looked askance at each other.

Mom twisted her mouth. "Okay, okay, time us if you want."

"I think it's a good idea, Dad," I said.

"Thank you," he replied. I wasn't sure if he was talking to me or to Mom. He got the timer on his phone ready.

We went to our positions in the yard. My heart pounded as I waited on the edge of the mud pit. I shook out my hands to try to relieve some tension, and I realized that my wrist hadn't bothered me in ages. I was feeling pretty good!

Every member of my family waited at their obstacle. We had all tried our best over the last few weeks. What had started off as a simple wish, for me to have the Summer of Fun and to train for Dominator Ninja, hadn't worked out as I had originally hoped. It had somehow turned out better.

With our hard work, we were going to finish the Soiled Pants obstacle race. For the first time in my whole life, I felt like there was no possible way I was going to screw this up. I had done the work and put in the time. We were going to make it to that finish line. Hopefully walk away with a medal around our necks and maybe, just maybe, a chance at a free membership to Agile Ninja Training Centre. That prize would be the ultimate — better than a confetti bomb. This future ninja had never been so prepared and so ready to get dirty.

22

THAT'S MY JAM

IT WAS VERY HARD TO TALK TO DAVEY AND AARON at the same time because of time zone differences. But we finally found a time that worked. Davey had been a bit annoyed at me for showing Aaron the backyard without him a few weeks ago when Aaron and I had FaceTimed, so I made sure to try to set up a time that worked for everybody to have the "big reveal" for my friends. Even though the yard had been set up for a couple of weeks already, they hadn't seen it all done yet.

After many texts back and forth, we finally settled on a date and a time: August 21 at 7 a.m. Vancouver time, 10 a.m. Barrie time, and 10 p.m. Shanghai time.

When my alarm went off at 6:45, I got up and splashed

water on my face. After a quick change out of my pajamas, I went outside and waited for 7 a.m.

Davey called first.

"Hey," he said.

I held out the iPad and greeted him.

"You've got an eye booger," he told me promptly. "Right side."

I picked at it and scrubbed my entire hand down my face.

"Nice to see you too," I laughed. "How's Shanghai?"

"It's so hot, every time we leave the apartment, I want to die."

"Come on." He had to be exaggerating.

"Like, as soon as the air hits your face, it feels like you're in an oven. The oven doesn't smell good, either." Davey waved his hand in front of his face.

"Traveling is fun though, isn't it? We haven't gone anywhere this summer."

"Fun? Are you kidding me? I was stuck on the tarmac in Shenzhen for two hours last week. No AC! You *must* be having more fun than me!"

I thought about it. "Well, *parts* of the summer have been fun." I was hoping that the end of it would be the most fun part though.

"That's more than I can say."

Aaron finally called and said, "So, show us the full course already!" He hadn't even said hello yet.

"Uh, *hi*." Davey waved.

"Hey. Come on, Ev! Get moving!" Aaron rolled his finger in the air, encouraging me to start.

"Okay, okay." I stood up and started to walk them through the course.

I did a quick tour of the yard — most of it they'd seen in bits and pieces already. Everything except the wall. When I finally showed them, they were duly impressed.

"Your dad built that for you?" Davey asked in disbelief.

"Not bad, right?"

"That's cool," Aaron agreed. "My dad doesn't even know what a hammer does."

"He's an accountant," I reminded him.

"So?" Aaron shrugged. "He's good with numbers. That means he should be able to use a tape measure."

Davey started cracking up.

"What's so funny?" I asked.

"You know how a lot of the people on Dominator Ninja have nicknames?" Davey asked as he tried to calm himself.

Aaron and I nodded. Some of the names were based on people's jobs or unusual things about them. There was Clean Sweep (dental hygienist), The Trucker (self-explanatory), and Strong Strong (a description and a last name). Come to think of it, there actually was a guy named The Accountant too.

"I just thought of yours." Davey peered closer into his screen, so all we could see were his lips.

"Lucky Break!"

Aaron groaned. "I mean, that's not really a ninja name. More like something he needs."

"Okay, okay, it sounded better in my head," Davey admitted. "But you are still pretty lucky."

"How am I lucky?" I asked. I knew Davey's grandmother was superstitious about lucky numbers, but was it lucky in Chinese culture to break bones and sprain wrists too?

"Your family is doing all this for you, you goof. My sister pretends I'm not even in the room most times," Davey answered. "She's such a diva." He rolled his eyes.

I pondered what it would be like to have Lydia and Georgia ignore me. That wouldn't be *too* bad, sometimes, would it?

"Yeah, my family makes me waste my whole summer sitting in a canoe. Nobody asks me what *I* want to do — ever!" Aaron said. "I'm learning how to make *jam*. I don't want to make jam!"

"But it's tasty, at least," I offered.

Aaron walked over to a wooden kitchen cupboard inside the cottage. There was an entire shelf full of jam.

"Nobody needs this much jam. I hate the sight of those wild raspberries. I'd give anything to do a Soiled Pants race with my family instead of sterilizing jars. We're supposed to can peaches today." He let out a huge sigh.

"Will you two be back in time to come to the event

and watch?" I asked. "Maybe bring your parents and convince them to join next time?"

Davey scoffed. "My mom only wears mud packs when she's in the spa. But I'll be back home by then. I'll try to get them to take me."

"Me too!" Aaron said.

"Thanks, guys. I'll text you the address and stuff. I'm pretty nervous," I admitted.

"Of course, but still. It looks like fun, and that's the most important thing." Davey held up his hand to the camera as soon as he finished talking. "Oh, wait, I got all serious for a sec. Like Mr. Humberton."

I hadn't thought about Mr. Humberton or his final fourth-grade assignment in a while. The Summer of Fun poster had become like wallpaper on the fridge now — my eye passed over it without really taking it in. But without that assignment, my summer would have been very different.

At the mention of Mr. Humberton, we laughed and reminisced about school. Then we talked about other things. Aaron showed us the canoe he hated so much. I thought it looked pretty fun. Davey walked us around his grandmother's apartment and showed us how busy traffic was outside the building.

After we said our goodbyes, I put the iPad down on my lap and glanced at the backyard again. I mean, I guess I *was* lucky, in a way.

23

RACE DAY

I WOKE UP AT THE CRACK OF DAWN. I HAD SLEPT restlessly because I had too much nervous energy surging through my body. Today was the day.

Eating breakfast was nearly impossible. I had no appetite, but I knew I should eat *something*. Plain rice fried with a scrambled egg was all I could manage.

Lydia came downstairs looking haggard and bleary. She held a bunch of T-shirts in her arms.

"Yellow?" I asked.

"Don't blame Lydia. They were all out of black at the craft store. Sorry," Mom said, sipping her coffee.

"What happened to being that tough Korean-Canadian family?" I asked. She passed one to me and I lifted it up to see that she had written *Team Park* in bubble lettering across the back of the tees in a gel ink that puffed up when it dried.

I personally would not have picked purple as my lettering color of choice, but I guess it didn't really matter. The shirt wouldn't stay yellow and purple for long.

"We're tough, in disguise." Lydia placed a piece of bread in the toaster and sat down next to me. "So, how are you feeling?"

"Pretty sure I might throw up." I rubbed my stomach.

"Before one of my meets, I always go somewhere quiet and just sit by myself."

"Ehbun! Come sit with me! I miss you!" Georgia yelled from upstairs.

"Did you ever sit on a *bathroom* floor before competing?" I asked.

Lydia smiled. "Just once. But then I medaled in uneven bars, so it turned out okay."

I wasn't really feeling put out by Georgia's request. She'd been a real trooper lately and was almost an expert at burpees.

"You've been doing great without me," I told her as I walked through the bathroom doorway. She was already sitting on the toilet.

"My tummy hurts," she complained.

"Do you have to . . . you know, poop?"

"Already did! Want to see?" Georgia pointed down into the bowl.

"No!" I said emphatically. I sat on the floor, a little farther away from her than I normally would have.

"Maybe you're just a little nervous. My tummy doesn't feel great either. That happens."

"Can you read me a book?"

"The usual?" I had long given up trying to pretend the hedgehog-and-unicorn book didn't exist.

"No, I want. . . . Oh no! Second-best book isn't here!" She looked behind her at the stack of books sitting on top of the tank.

"Can you accept a replacement? How about your third-favorite book?"

She scrunched up her face. "Umm . . . Mommy said to try new book. New things can be fun." She passed me an unfamiliar book from the pile.

"That's our summer motto." I smiled. After I glanced at the book cover, I could see that this one likely had no talking animals! I opened it up and started to read.

I stared out the window as we drove to Bear Creek Park and tried not to barf. The Soiled Pants: Family Edition event was set up in what is normally a huge grassy field. I could see the fencing around the racecourse from the road, but I couldn't see what was *inside* the fence because it was completely covered in banners and advertisements.

"Oh, I wish we could see inside!" I complained as Dad parked. I wondered if Davey and Aaron were here yet, but probably not. But I'd keep looking for them.

"It will look just like the pictures on their website, I'm sure," Dad said.

"It had better." Lydia blew a giant bubble.

We filed out of the car, and I stared at the fencing that was blocking my view of the course. It built up the suspense, that was for sure. Right now, I hated suspense.

We followed the signs that said "Competitors' Entrance/Check-in." There were several tables set up and the staff wore matching orange Soiled Pants jackets. Once people checked in, they were given numbered stickers for their T-shirts. After the stickers were adhered, the staff let participants in through the gate.

Things went pretty quickly because each group moved through together. I was grateful for the speed, as I was about to chew my thumbnail off completely. It wasn't long before Team Park was next up at the registration table.

Mom handled everything silently and passed everyone their stickers.

A staff member, a wiry-looking woman with a high blond ponytail, ran through a checklist with us.

"Okay, Team Park. Here's some important information. The event starts precisely at 11 a.m. Also, we were starting to receive some feedback from some repeat contestants that they were growing a bit tired of the same course we'd been using over the last few years, so this season we are introducing new events for this race! Isn't that amazing news?"

I felt a lump in my throat. *No, no, no,* I thought.

I glanced over at Lydia, whose mouth was wide open with surprise too.

"New events?" Dad blurted out.

"Oh yes!" the staff member smiled. "I think you'll find the new obstacles exciting and fresh."

I didn't want *exciting* and *fresh*! I would have gladly settled for predictable and stale. "What are they? The new events?" I squeaked. We had planned! We had practiced! Was it all in vain?

"Oh, you'll see once you're inside," the staff member said mysteriously. Then her face turned serious. She continued, "Between now and the official start time, you may browse the new obstacle course, but you *may not touch anything.* I repeat. You may not touch *anything.* No practicing, no testing. Anybody caught using the equipment will be asked to withdraw."

I was starting to lose feeling in my legs.

She wasn't even done. "At each station, there is an official to ensure that you are playing fair and completing the obstacle correctly. The next member of your team may only start their obstacle with a hand slap from the member before them. If you fail to complete the obstacle a staff member will escort you off the racecourse. Each member must complete one obstacle individually, the only exception being the sixth and final obstacle: *Wall of Doom*. We usually end with a wall, but this year's wall is modified from previous years. You'll see."

Dad looked at me nervously. But I let out a sigh of relief. At least there was still a wall. We had practiced that. So not *everything* was different.

"Every member must clear that last obstacle in order to successfully finish the race. Here is your final form. After you do your walk-through, please fill in which member will be doing each event and return it to an official, wearing a jacket like mine."

She finally breathed and handed Mom a small cardboard card and a golf pencil. "And lastly . . ."

There was *more*?

"As you can see, the top three families will be awarded these medals." She stepped out of the way and pointed to a display cabinet she had been standing in front of. "Aren't they sweet?"

I almost salivated. These were the quirkiest, funniest-looking gold, silver, and bronze medals I had ever seen. Instead of a traditional circular medal, these looked like rippling pools of mud — slightly irregular in shape and with a pair of shorts sticking out of the middle. I wanted one. I wanted one a lot.

"How many other teams are entered?" I asked.

She glanced down at her clipboard. "Fourteen teams in total. And did you know, Vancouver is so lucky to have Agile Ninja Training Centre opening next week. They have graciously donated a yearlong family membership to one lucky family that finishes the race! That prize is specific only to this event at this location! That award will be selected in a random draw depending on who finishes the race."

She pointed to the training center's advertisement banner on a stand that was gently flapping in the breeze.

"So, you *have* to finish?" Mom asked.

"Well, for that particular draw, yes."

"Do lots of people *not* finish?" Lydia asked.

"Unfortunately, some people don't come into the event seriously. They just think it'll be a fun morning. Don't get me wrong, it *is* fun! But you have to have prepared to be able to finish. All clear?"

As clear as . . . mud. My mind was in a daze with all this information. We had new, untested events to deal with. There were thirteen other families all vying for cool medals *and* a chance for a free family membership to Agile Ninja Training Centre. I gulped.

"Good to go!" Georgia shouted.

I knew in my heart of hearts that we had prepared. We had done our best, anyway. But still, I felt like I was going to soil my pants. Literally.

24

THE UNEXPECTED

THE SOILED PANTS ORGANIZERS WERE PRETTY serious about keeping the course a secret. After the check-in, the fencing herded us like cattle through a zigzagged path. Finally, past all the covered fencing, the main obstacle course field was visible.

I stopped dead in my tracks and took it all in.

At one end of the field, close to the finish line, there was a small set of bleachers. While not a lot of spectators had arrived yet, there were enough people to make some noise. There was a very large contingent for a team called Team Sidhu's Plumbing chanting "Plumbers get it done! Plumbers get it done!" They stood out because of their use of PVC piping to hold their signs.

Then I saw them. Aaron and Davey. I waved at them, hoping to catch their attention. When they noticed me, they lifted a large Korean flag with a scrap of fabric attached. It might have been an old pillowcase. On the fabric, they had spray-painted *Team Park*. I cracked a smile, and they jumped around and waved it some more.

I gave them a thumbs-up and felt happy that my friends had taken time during the last weekend of the summer to come cheer me on. It felt nice that Team Park had our own cheering section. It would be even better if they could watch me *win*.

As happy as I was to see them, I couldn't let my friends distract me. It was time to focus. I needed to inspect the rest of the venue. If you looked quickly, it appeared exactly like the pictures from the website. But I wasn't fooled. I knew they had thrown in unexpected twists. I hated twists.

There was a large board with the names of the events. Many contestants were already standing in front of it reading and planning with their teams.

I read the board.

#1. Balance These Logs
#2. Spin It Good
#3. TIREd Yet?
#4. Traverse This
#5. Come Crawling Home
#6. Wall of Doom

Immediately, I got a bad feeling about these events.

"I don't think there's even a mud pit!" I yelled.

"No *Boulder over the Shoulder!*" Dad exclaimed.

Georgia started to cry. "That was the best one!"

Mom squatted down to comfort her. "*Shhh*, it's okay! It will still be fun!"

"I'm starting to have my doubts about that," Lydia grumbled.

"Come on! It could still be fun!" I exclaimed, trying to convince myself just as much as Lydia. "Let's keep going with the walk-through."

Over each obstacle there was a big banner with a number and the name of the obstacle. We headed toward number one.

Balance These Logs.

With my hands on my hips, I took in the structure. One thing about living in British Columbia is the trees. Lots of trees. Big trees. The whole province is practically a giant forest. Logs were a part of life here.

It started off with rows of logs, hovering above the ground, placed in such a way that you had to run across the top of them. There seemed to be different paths to take in order to make it to the end. Under the logs, a sloppy-looking slick of mud. Okay, so there *was* mud. Just not what I was expecting.

Then after this section of flat logs there were stumps. Log stumps. A bunch of them spaced out. There was more mud here too. I felt like whooping with relief. I was practically a log stump expert!

"This event is all mine!" I exclaimed. After a few moments of sheer panic that all our training and planning was going to be useless, I suddenly felt good. I never thought the sight of mud could be so comforting and calming.

Obstacle number two was *Spin It Good.*

Georgia ran ahead to this next start area. She squealed and raised a fist. "Go Peloton!"

I moved quicker. Could it be? A bicycle-themed obstacle? It's like the gods of luck and fortune were smiling down on my family right now.

"Can you believe this?" Mom exclaimed.

This obstacle *did* involve cycling — specifically, sitting at a stationary bike and pedaling your face off. The pedaling propelled a conveyor belt that moved you forward. While traveling along the conveyor belt, it appeared, judging by the presence of small catapults and buckets of mud along the side of the conveyor belt, you got pelted with mud. It was best to hurry.

Lydia laughed. "This is totally bonkers! Mom, this one is all for you!"

Mom looked pleased and relieved. "I'm not the best cyclist yet, but definitely better than I was at the start of the summer. Also picking up all those toys sure helped my leg strength."

Dad looked glum and pouted. "What am *I* going to do?"

"Come on." I nudged him along. "Let's go see the third obstacle."

TIREd Yet?

Based on the name, it sounded, just for a moment, like it might be an event that involved lifting tires. I had high hopes. I think Dad did too. It would have been the perfect event for him. But this is where our luck ran out.

There were tires all right, but lifting wasn't part of the obstacle. There was the classic layout of tires on the ground, arranged in slightly askew rows. You had to put a single foot in each tire and race through as fast as you could, while still stepping inside each tire. But these tires were weirdly thick. There was going to be some serious high knee action involved in getting your feet in and out of these tires.

The next part looked even more difficult. There were five tires in a row, suspended from a rope, each tire higher than the next. You had to climb *through* them. The first one was pretty low to the ground, easy enough to get through, but the tires kept getting higher and higher. By the fifth tire, you might need to fly to pass through it.

Dad's eyes got wide when he saw how high the final tire was. "Uh, I don't think this one's for me," he said.

It wasn't Georgia's event either. The last three tires were clearly above her head.

"Lydia?" I asked. "Can you do this one?"

She shrugged indifferently. "Sure."

We moved to the next obstacle.

Traverse This.

"A *water pit*?" I spat. I looked up to the sky. Why did they suddenly have to copy Dominator Ninja?

There were long ropes hammered into the ground at the start, and the end of the rope was anchored to a raised platform. You needed to climb the length of the rope to get to the platform. The angle made it extra challenging. I could see that anybody on this obstacle would have their back to the ground the whole time while trying to get to the platform. It wasn't even really rope *climbing*. Clinging like a lemur would have been a better description.

From the flat platform, if you even made it that far, the goal was to make it to the *other* platform, across the water pit. The only way across — more ropes. There were horizontal ropes suspended across the length of the water pit. There were ropes down low, probably to step and walk across, and some ropes up high, probably good for holding to keep your balance. But this part of the obstacle was clearly a delicate and tricky high-wire act.

Everybody looked at Dad. My very burly dad.

Dad looked nervously to Lydia. "Want to change?"

"Why don't we just see what the last obstacle is before we make any final decisions," Lydia said wisely.

Lydia, I knew, could pretty much do anything she set her mind to. She could handle this event. It was the other two I was worried about. Dad had been counting on an event where brute strength was involved. He was out of luck so far. And what about Georgia? What on earth was a *toddler* supposed to do?

There were no clear and obvious choices yet. But the name of the last obstacle gave me some hope.

Come Crawling Home.

Once I took in the whole view and this final individual event became clear, I regained some optimism. The *Sticky Spiderweb Net* was supposed to be Georgia's thing. This last individual obstacle wasn't the same thing at all, and in some ways, it was the exact opposite.

Instead of the rope obstacle being set up vertically, the ropes of this event were suspended in a horizontal plane, hovering about a foot above the ground. It forced you to crawl *under* the ropes, which were crisscrossed in a tight diamond pattern. Once you were down on the ground, you had to stay down.

The ropes started out wide enough for at least four or five people to start crawling together. Then the passageway narrowed, like a funnel. You could only escape one at a time.

Because this event was low to the ground and best suited for small people, how could I not be happy seeing this?

"Georgia. This one's yours." I crouched down slightly to give her my full attention. She usually liked that. "Doesn't it look *great*?" I asked, with added enthusiasm.

She wasn't smiling.

"I like going *up*." She pointed to the sky. "Sticky Spiderweb!"

"You can pretend you're going *up* the ground!" I suggested.

"How dumb do you think I am?" Georgia asked. "That's crawling."

I gave up. I could only keep up the chipper children's librarian voice for so long. "Well, too bad, it's your event."

"Well, Dad, that leaves *TIREd Yet?* or *Traverse This*," Lydia said. "You pick what you want."

Dad considered his choices but didn't answer. Instead, he just twisted his mouth.

Lydia cleared her throat. "Mom? You know Dad best. You're committed life partners, after all. What do *you* think?" Lydia's voice was light and full of innocence.

Mom looked startled at the direct question. She glanced furtively at Dad.

"Well," Mom said, looking uncomfortable. "If I had to choose . . ."

"And we *do* need to make a decision and write it down," Lydia said calmly, pointing to the card we were given at the registration desk.

Mom exhaled loudly. "The tire thing."

"It *is* the lesser of two evils," Dad agreed. "I think I could climb the rope up to make it to the platform, but

I don't think I could keep my balance the whole length of the rope over the water."

"That's what I thought," Mom said suddenly, with her face slightly animated.

I watched my parents talk. It might have been the first thing they had agreed on in a long time. The unexpected events could have really caused a lot of problems with morale. But instead of causing tension, these new events seemed to be bringing us closer together. It was surprising, and honestly, a relief. Any cracks in Team Park were being patched together by a muddy field and maybe a tiny bit of fear.

"Okay. I'll do *TIREd Yet?*" he said with determination. I was glad to hear it, because just a moment ago, I had been afraid that he had lost his fighting spirit. He nodded his head a few times and said to himself, "I can do it."

"Okay, it's settled," I said.

Mom started writing down names on the card, and now that that was decided, I apprehensively started checking out the other contestants, many of whom had gathered by the final obstacle. The *Wall of Doom*.

Cue the dramatic music — that sucker was no joke.

25

RETURN OF THE NINJA

I WONDERED IF THE ORGANIZERS FOR SOILED
Pants had forgotten that today's race was a *family edition*.
The wall was *not* like the wall Dad had built in the backyard
at all. This was a wall built for people who could levitate.

I stood at the base of the wall and bent my neck to
look all the way up to the top. It was tall and straight. No
curve or bend like the classic warped wall in ninja courses.
No ropes to help you climb. Just a solid piece of flat, ridiculously high wood. We were used to twelve feet. This was
not twelve feet. Whatever height it was, it totally sucked.

When the perky staff person had told us all about the
changes they'd made to the course, I had done a good job
holding it all together in the face of having my well laid-
out plans utterly destroyed. But now, as I contemplated

how much I loathed the sight of this wall, I began to feel my spirits crumbling. This wall seemed impossible. I was starting to feel lost and hopeless when a familiar voice drifted across the obstacle field.

"Evan?"

I turned my head in the direction of the voice and there he was — Darren.

Both of our faces lit up once we recognized each other.

Darren sprinted toward us. As soon as he was within reach, Darren asked, "Bear hug?"

I nodded and before I knew it, I was in the air.

"I'm so excited to see you here!" Darren exclaimed, swinging me around.

"You're working here?" I asked, looking at Darren's orange event jacket.

"Yes! But I'm also doing the regular team event with some buddies tomorrow," Darren said.

I laughed. Of course he was.

"Well, Evan Park, seems your wrist has recovered very nicely, and you took my advice," Darren said.

"You *are* an excellent physiotherapist."

"I like this kid," Darren said, pointing at me while looking at my family. "What's your team's name?"

"Team Park." I turned to show him the back of my shirt.

"Come on," Darren said, feigning frustration. "You can do better than *that*. Let's hear it from your belly."

"Team Park," I squeaked alone. I raised a fist but quickly brought it down.

Darren sighed. "Okay, first rule of a Soiled Pants obstacle race: if you don't have hype, you'd better go home."

"Where are the car keys?" Mom said, patting her pockets.

Darren looked her up and down inquisitively. "I didn't know you had such a sense of humor."

"I like Darren," Georgia said enthusiastically.

"I'm likeable!" he replied. "Come on. You need to shout your team's name like you mean it." Darren's testosterone was pumping. I could smell it.

Darren slapped his hands together and said with increased intensity, "Say it like you mean it! Put your hands in." With his energy surging, he was hard to ignore. Team Park made a circle, and everyone put one hand in. "I'm going to ask you again! What's your team's name?" Darren held his left hand open behind his ear.

"Team Park!" we all shouted while we tossed our hands up to the sky.

Darren leaned into me. He held my gaze firmly but with a softness that didn't make me want to turn away. "Remember when I first met you? You couldn't write your name clearly with a pencil."

I remembered. It seemed like such a long time ago. Darren continued, "No matter what happens out there, you've got nothing to prove to anybody but yourself. And you've got a lot to be proud of."

I felt flushed and nodded before I swallowed hard.

"Now, go out there and try not to hurt yourselves!" Darren said loudly to the entire family. He turned to leave but quickly turned back. "Second rule? Have fun." Darren smiled mischievously and jogged away.

"Who *was* that guy?" Dad asked, confused.

Mom looked away and tried not to laugh.

"Oh, right, you never met him before." I chuckled. "He was the physiotherapist for my wrist."

"If you think about it, he's kind of the reason we're here," Lydia said.

"So, this is all *his* fault," Dad said quietly.

Georgia squeezed her father's leg. "Daddy's funny today."

Mom and I side-eyed each other and tried not to laugh.

"Come on, Dad!" Lydia slapped his upper arm. "I thought you'd love this!"

"I guess . . ." He faltered. "I wasn't prepared. I had imagined things differently."

I knew exactly what Dad was talking about. "Me too. But we have to adapt, be flexible."

I expected her to do it, and she didn't let me down. Georgia bent over and touched her forehead to her knees. I patted her back. "Yes, you are very flexible."

Now that we had submitted our list to the organizers, there was no going back. The only thing left was to wait for start time and stress about how we were going to get up the *Wall of Doom*.

"How are we going to scale that thing?" Dad muttered.

"I don't think we'll know until we're in front of it," Lydia said.

"Maybe we can watch how other teams do it. I think there must be some experienced competitors. You know, families that have done this kind of thing before. That's why they changed things up," Mom said.

I found myself scowling. The families that *complained*. The families that ruined my plans. I wondered if I'd be able to spot them in the crowd. They'd be walking around with a bit more confidence than newbies like us.

There were lots of kids around, but not lots of *little* kids. Mostly ten and older, some old enough that I wondered why they hadn't entered the *regular* race! Some people would go to any lengths to win.

Most teams had their own custom tees. Team Sidhu's Plumbing was wearing blue, and they were unique because of the boys of the same height and stocky build. Teenage *triplets*. The boys menacingly banged together copper pipes. I gulped.

But there was one team that really stood out. They wore orange and looked to be family members of the Dutch national volleyball team — all practically giants. If

there was a kid on this team, they were disguising themselves as a semipro athlete. I couldn't read their tees, so
mentally I called them Team Gouda.

"We're definitely going to get passed by *them*," Lydia
whispered to me after observing the team of Dutch giants.

Silently, I agreed with her. But still, I couldn't get the
image of the cool medals out of my head, despite the over-
whelming height of Team Gouda.

I started to check out the other teams standing near
us. A few other teams caught my eye. Like Team Say
No to Climate Change in matching green tees. They
seemed to have an environmentally responsible grandmother in their mix, plus a girl about Lydia's age. I
thought that they seemed beatable.

Team Martin's Used Cars in black tees had a stiff-
looking member, maybe an aunt, and a young boy,
maybe eight. A young kid. That was good. We could beat
them too.

I couldn't really check out anybody else carefully, as
the teams were spread too far apart. There were thirteen
other teams we needed to beat, and that's all I needed
to know.

A piercing whistle sounded, followed by an amplified
voice over speakers, "The race starts in ten minutes. Please
head to your obstacle."

26

THE SWEET SPOT

AFTER SEEING DARREN, I HAD TO GET MY GAME face back on. I slapped myself randomly in multiple places. It helped calm my nerves. My shoulders, my arms, my calves, my chest. I bonked myself on my forehead a few times too. I stopped hearing the crowd and focused on the task at hand.

Team Park, like everybody else, had spread out to the starting lines of their various obstacles. Since Georgia's event was the last individual event, Lydia was going to stay with her until Mom or I could make our way to her after completing our turns, and then Lydia could hustle over to her starting line.

A jumping figure off the edge of the course caught my eye. Darren was wildly gesturing, and I finally looked his way. He brought his two index fingers up to his face and drew a smile in the air.

I was thankful for his reminder and gave Darren a smile. I pushed a big breath of air out of my nose when I realized I had just spent the last few minutes wondering how to beat everybody else, silently hoping that other teams would crash and burn.

Obviously, I hadn't found that competitive sweet spot Lydia told me about. The most important thing about being here was supposed to be to compete while doing my best *and* have fun at the same time. I sighed in frustration. The sweet spot was very hard to reach.

I didn't know why a grandmother and a stiff-looking aunt would come to an event like this. It certainly wasn't to win. But if I could guess, they probably wanted to do just one thing: they wanted to come out here and give it everything they had to show themselves something, all while having fun with their family. That was the ninja way.

Really, that's all I wanted too. The medals and winning that gym membership would be great — I wouldn't say *no* to any of that! — but first, I needed to say *yes* to fun.

I placed my toe up against the yellow starting line. My foot twitched anxiously. *Smile. Enjoy it,* I told myself. Finally, the whistle sounded, and I was off. I focused in on the logs — nothing else. From where I had stood before, during the walk-through, I hadn't seen the big gaps between the rows. This obstacle forced me to do some serious jumping.

From the corner of my eye, I could see I was being passed by some racers. I couldn't even think about it. I needed to worry about my own speed and keeping my own balance.

I found myself saying "Whoa!" more than once, bending at the waist and flailing my arms to keep steady. Had they covered the logs with some kind of grease?

Then I heard the first victim of the slippery logs.

Splat into the muddy ground right behind me. I dared not look behind, but it was enough for me to lose my concentration. And that's all it took. I stumbled.

"Oof," I grunted as my chest came slamming down against a log. As a survival reflex, I clamped my limbs around the log and held on with everything I had.

"Get up, Evan!" Mom yelled from her spot at the start of the next obstacle.

Did she honestly think I wanted to stay down?

I could not respond because the wind had been knocked out of me, but I was still *on* the obstacle. That was good news. Not like that poor guy next to me who was struggling to get out of the mud underneath the log and climb back up on the course.

Carefully, I got back on my feet. I was almost there. The stumps were within view.

One foot in front of the other, I told myself. The slip had taken a little spring out of my step, and I was more cautious than I wanted to be, but still, I moved forward.

Now the stumps.

I wasn't going to take anything for granted. I was going to land on each one, and I was going to take my time.

The sight of two other contestants passing by did not faze me.

The stumps were not aligned in any particular way. Some were placed close together, some were not. Just like I'd practiced at home. I leapt and landed and then jumped again. I swallowed hard. The next stump was pretty far away, but I thought I could do it.

As I leapt, I suddenly wasn't sure I could come to a complete stop on the stump, as I had with the others. I panicked mid-air, and in a fraction of a second, made the decision to simply use this stump like a springboard to the final landing platform, like a quick tap dance. As soon as my right foot hit the top of the stump, I pushed off as hard as I could and leapt toward the platform. I landed in a heap in front of Mom, who was waiting to start her turn.

I slapped Mom's hand, and, just like that, my turn was over. I'd done it.

I didn't have time to dwell on anything. Mechanically, I picked myself up. I needed to get to Georgia's obstacle so that Lydia could get to hers.

I ran along the side of Mom's obstacle. She was pedaling like a video cycling instructor was threatening her very existence. Then the mud catapults started. Luckily,

I dodged a few wads flying across the course on my way down to where Georgia and Lydia were waiting.

"Go, Mom!" I shouted as I passed her. She was holding her own and staying in about the middle of the pack.

Hunched over the handlebars of the bike, Mom did not reply.

I ran past the staging area for Dad's event and flexed my bicep as a show of strength. Dad slapped his chest in return.

I kept running. As soon as Lydia saw me, she sprinted to her starting line.

As our paths crossed, we high-fived each other without breaking our strides.

By the time I reached Georgia, I was completely out of breath.

Georgia grabbed at my leg and squeezed it nervously. Team Gouda had already finished *TIREd Yet?* and, from out of nowhere, Team Say No to Climate Change seemed to charge into second place. Clearly, they had an advantage in the *Spin It Good* event because they probably cycled everywhere.

However, Team Martin's Used Cars seem to falter and fell behind Mom. I bet nobody on that team even owned a bicycle.

Georgia and I stared down the field and watched Mom, covered in only a few clumps of mud, slap Dad's hand. It was his turn.

He let out a mighty roar before he ran. I could even hear it from here!

Feeling like a bundle of nerves about to pop, I watched Dad negotiate the unusually thick tires. One foot in, followed by a slightly awkward moment when Dad seemed to doubt his ability to lift his free leg high enough to put it into the next tire.

"Stretch!" Georgia screamed.

Dad, realizing his limits, resorted to lifting his free leg with his hands and stiffly repeating the task until he was clear of the last tire. He had managed to finish this section, even if it didn't look pretty. And it *really* hadn't been pretty.

Now the hard part. The five tires, suspended in the air like giant donuts in the sky, waited. I watched other participants tackle these tires. There were two different styles: the *let's gracefully float through them, like a circus acrobat* approach and the *let's squeeze through them and crash on the ground* approach.

Dad fit into only one of these groups.

Surprisingly, he managed to pass through the first three tires without difficulty. He didn't look *graceful,* but he had managed. It was the fourth tire hanging at shoulder height that was the problem.

I recoiled when I saw Dad wriggle through and hit the ground with his left shoulder first. It was hard not to wince with sympathy. "That had to hurt," I said to Georgia.

"Daddy's tough!" Georgia yelled. "Do it again!"

On the last excruciating tire, Dad had to jump up as high as he could and wedge his torso into the hole. He swung in the air while he muscled his way through the tire. But on the exit, Dad's shoe caught on the rubber, leaving him hanging for a split second. He looked even more awkward than he'd been on the previous tires. His weight eventually dragged him down, and he landed hard on his left shoulder, again.

He howled in pain and made a grab for it with his right hand.

I brought my hands up to my face. "Oh, boy."

Lydia was gesturing wildly for Dad to stand and just finish. Urging him on, her hands turned like a rotisserie chicken oven on high-speed.

Grimacing and covered in dirt, Dad got up and slapped Lydia's hand before collapsing. He was in second-to-last place.

"Is Daddy hurt?" Georgia asked quietly.

"I hope not," I said, watching Dad, who was visibly struggling.

Dad heaved a few big breaths before hauling his hobbled body down the field. He looked like a warrior. I felt so proud of him because it would have been so easy to quit. But he didn't. He knew he had to join Mom at the base of the *Wall of Doom*. He knew we needed him.

Team Gouda and Team Say No to Climate Change and several others started the *Come Crawling Home* section of the race. The crowd of spectators cheered, and some rang handbells frantically. I didn't want any distractions, so I didn't even look for Aaron and Davey in the crowd.

I had taken my eyes off Lydia to make sure Dad was okay, and by the time I found her again, she was almost finished. I watched her hop off the last section of rope.

Before I knew it, she was right in front of me. She had left many competitors in the dust.

"Are you waiting for a personal invitation?" Lydia held her hand open for Georgia.

Georgia slapped it and turned to face her event.

27

NEGOTIATIONS

GEORGIA JUST STOOD THERE FOR A MOMENT.

"Crawl, Georgia! Crawl!" Lydia and I shouted, pointing down to the ground. One of the Sidhu triplets passed Georgia.

She looked offended. "I'm three. And a half! I'm not a baby!"

Oh, *now* she was suddenly too old to crawl. Talk about a terrible time to develop *pride*. I suppressed my frustration and channeled my inner magician.

I looked her deep in the eyes. "Yes, you are a very big girl." I was trying a monotone voice to induce Georgia into a trance-like state. "But sometimes, isn't it fun to crawl?"

All the noise — the screaming, the shouting — I couldn't hear it anymore. It was just me trying to convince an unpredictable toddler to crawl under a grid made of rope suspended a foot above the ground. This was the biggest challenge of my life. I deserved *all* the medals.

Two more competitors flung themselves to the ground and started crawling.

"Sometimes," she agreed.

"Isn't it nice when all the mud gets squishy in your fingers? Try it." I crouched, scooped some mud, and passed it to her.

"Squishy!" she said, clasping her hands together.

"If you crawl to the end, under all this rope, you can squish mud in my face!" I was already dirty, what did I care? "Won't that be fun?"

The smallest of smiles started to emerge in the corners of Georgia's mouth. "Yes," she admitted.

Many of the contestants had already finished this portion of the race. There was only Georgia and two others left. Any lead Lydia had regained was lost at this point.

Of the last two remaining competitors, one of them, probably the mother of one family, looked like she was spry and easily motivated, but the other one seemed to be a disinterested older teen who, judging by his slouchy shoulders, didn't even want to be here.

By now, I knew we weren't going to win. But suddenly, I was okay with that. I had to be. Even with this realization, I felt strangely calm. Now, I just wanted us to finish.

"Ready!" I said energetically to Georgia. I wasn't sure where I was finding all this enthusiasm. I'd heard Dad talk about athletes *digging deep,* and this was digging of the epic variety.

I plunked myself down in the mud. "Like this!" I demonstrated to Georgia.

A ref blew a whistle at me. "No! It's *her* turn!"

I threw the ref an evil glare. "I'm helping her. She's *three.* Geez. Cut the three-year-old some slack, would you?"

The ref put down the whistle. "Okay, but rules are rules. All team members must do at least one obstacle by themselves. It's only fair."

I turned back to Georgia, who had finally joined me on the ground. "Okay, use your elbows and launch yourself forward under the rope. Got it?"

Georgia nodded. "Then Ehbun eats mud pie."

I got up and yelled, "Go!"

I watched my little sister blow by the disinterested teen. Georgia's little elbows plunged into the ground, one after another, and propelled her forward.

Lydia and my parents waited at the *Wall of Doom.* They were all screaming at the top of their lungs. It was strange how a little mud, and several obstacles that made you work much harder than necessary, could turn even the most mild-mannered person into a shouting fanatic.

Speaking of fanatics, I was close enough to the bleachers now to easily catch a glimpse of Aaron and Davey, who looked possessed. Aaron had taken off his shirt and was spinning it over his head.

My attention went back to my sister. I waited for her, flat on my stomach. "Come on, Georgia! You can do it. Almost there!"

"That mud pie is going to be yummy," she giggled.

I smacked my lips excessively. "I can't wait to taste it!"

I got up and gave her space to emerge from under the rope.

My entire family was jumping up and down. Georgia grabbed two fistfuls of mud and said, "Lunch time!"

I leaned forward and let Georgia smash the mud into my face.

It was foul, but I smiled with mud in my teeth. "Way to go!" I picked her up and swung her around.

"This is no time for a victory dance!" Dad shouted. He pointed at the wall.

Georgia said, "Can we just go *around* it?"

"Kind of defeats the purpose." I spat out a little mud before I glanced over and watched several other teams as they attempted to scale the wall.

It was high enough that even if tall people stood on each other's shoulders it was not guaranteed that they'd be able to grab the top edge with their fingertips. What chance did an average Korean family have? Even if you could reach the top, you'd need a pretty impressive amount of core strength to be able to swing your legs up and over.

Several teams could *almost* make it using this strategy, but I only saw one team actually manage it easily. The only successful group? Of course, it was Team Gouda.

"Georgia!" Dad shouted. "Climb onto Daddy's back!"

He squatted and she jumped up.

"There is no way we're tall enough for that tactic," I said.

"Stand on my shoulders," Dad insisted. "Let's try."

Mom said, "I don't think that's a good idea."

Georgia was on top of Dad's shoulders for about two seconds before he growled in annoyance. "Ow, ow, ow, Georgia, get off." She slid back to the ground. "I hit the ground funny, and it still hurts like crazy."

There was no person better suited on Team Park to be the base, the foundation of a human pyramid than Dad — when he was *healthy*. I didn't know how we were going to manage now.

We stood around hopelessly searching for a strategy. Dad, in particular, stared at the ground intensely with his jaw as tight as I'd ever seen it.

Suddenly, Dad slapped his forehead. "Huddle!" he barked.

We had never huddled before, and nobody knew what to do.

Dad waved his good arm and motioned for us to come to a circle. We put our heads in the middle of the huddle. Everybody was huffing, dirty, and focused.

"Why didn't I think of this sooner!" His eyes became enormous. "The lineout!"

His excitement was met with blank stares.

"From rugby!" he exclaimed. "Doesn't anybody pay attention when I'm talking?"

"Dad, it's time to accept that none of us are interested in your high school rugby stories," Lydia replied.

Dad sighed and then refocused. "You'll be interested in this! Listen! The lineout is when the props lift the hooker."

"Watch your language," Mom scolded.

I heard the roar of cheers. A team must have made it over the wall, but I stayed in the huddle and didn't look up.

Dad carried on. "In rugby, the biggest, strongest players lift lighter, smaller players into the air to catch a ball. If you do it right, the light person goes flying up into the air."

Lydia shrugged, "Okay, so then what?"

"You can grab the wall. You'll go higher than by standing on my shoulders. Which you can't do right now, anyway . . ." Dad explained. "Ev, you go first. Trust me. You'll go flying. Once you're over the top and steady on the platform on the other side, lean back over the wall. You have to help Georgia. She'll never be able to make it over otherwise."

Georgia pouted indignantly.

Dad broke our huddle. He looked at Mom and motioned her over to the wall. "We have to face each other, like this. Evan, you be stiff as a board. I'll grab your shorts; Mom will grab your calves. Then we hoist you up. I think my shoulder can handle this move."

Mom looked unsure as she squatted and grabbed my calves just above my ankles. This was not only weird but also bordering on uncomfortable.

I felt very unhappy with the idea of Dad using my shorts as the method for hoisting me into the air. It felt like a wedgie was probably inevitable in this situation.

"Ev, you need to reach straight up and grab the wall. Keep your back straight," Dad said, gripping the fabric near the waistband of my shorts into a tight fist. Then he turned to Mom and said calmly, "We need to work as a team. A unit. Like we used to be, remember? I know it's been a while . . . But if our timing is off, this won't work."

I saw one side of Mom's mouth form a deep crease, but she nodded.

I braced for a wedgie while Dad gave Mom further instructions about using her legs and not her back to lift. The cheers from the crowd faded away and I focused on the wall.

Before I knew it, I heard "Three!" and I was tossed in the air. Dad was right. It felt like I was flying. I shot my arms straight up and concentrated on the top edge of the wall. Then I grabbed it. My fingers curled over the top and I hung in the air. Miraculously, I was wedgie-free.

"Swing your legs over!" Lydia screamed.

My survival instincts kicked in. I knew my wrist hadn't built enough of its strength back to lift my dead weight straight up and over. I needed to swing my body like a pendulum for momentum. That would be the only way I could throw my leg over the side.

This all needed to happen quickly. I was losing strength in my fingers. I pumped my legs from side to side. My torso twisted. There was probably only one shot before I lost my grip.

I knew it was probable I was going to fall at any second. I knew that at this point, the best we could do was to just finish the race. But these past few minutes, with my face covered in mud, racing across wooden obstacles and working hard with my family to achieve this seemingly unimportant task of scaling a ridiculous wall, was the happiest I had ever felt.

I wanted to be happy just a few minutes more. So, without any hesitation, I put everything I had, every last bit of strength, into one final leg stretch, hoping that somehow, my body would cooperate.

It did. My running shoe was on top of the wall. My foot was taking pressure off of my very tired fingers and my slightly achy wrist and forearms. I muscled my leg just a bit farther over the wall until my entire calf was clear on the other side.

Below, my family jumped and applauded.

"Ev! You did it! You did it exactly right!" Dad cheered.

It was the first time he'd ever said that to me. But I didn't have time to dwell on it.

I was relieved as I collapsed onto the platform. It spanned the whole length of the wall, with stairs on two sides to exit. A solid piece of flat wood had never felt so good to stand on. I leaned over the wall and yelled, "Send her up!"

Georgia got into position. As easy as could be, Mom and Dad launched her into the air. I caught her arms and brought her onto the platform.

"Whee! Fun!" Georgia proclaimed.

"Who's next?" I yelled.

There was some discussion down below.

I glanced over at the team with the disinterested teenager. They were using the human pyramid strategy and finding some success. They had two members over.

"Send Mom!" I yelled.

Lydia hadn't done this move yet. She looked worried, but I was sure she could manage it.

I braced myself to help catch Mom. Even with her outstretched hands, only her right hand caught the top of the wall. As fast as I could, I reached over and grabbed her left arm.

My wrist twinged and I cursed loudly. With my body pressed up against the side of the wall, I knew to switch grips immediately and locked elbows with Mom instead. My wrist wouldn't be able to do much more.

"Get your leg up!" I said through gritted teeth.

"I'm trying," she replied breathlessly.

"Go Peloton!" Georgia screamed. "This ain't going to kill you yet! You got this!"

"Do *not* let go!" I shouted, securing my elbow as firmly as possible, all while trying to help her get over. "Move your body! Whatever it takes!"

"Mommy, climb!" Georgia screamed.

Mom, to her credit, did not give up when the two of us started yelling at her. With a fighting spirit that must have been ignited by video cycling coaches who encouraged by insulting, Mom found her last bit of energy. With a mighty primal growl, she propelled herself over the wall. The momentum pushed me on to my backside.

"Mommy!" Georgia smothered herself over Mom.

"That's some growl you've got there," I teased.

There was little time to cheer. Team Park was still two people down, and Dad's rugby-inspired strategy required three people for a successful launch over the wall. The math wasn't working anymore. I peered down at Lydia and Dad.

"Now what?"

Lydia said something to Dad. I saw his head tilt to the side, unsure.

I glanced at the racecourse. It was almost completely clear of competitors. It was just us, and the team with the disinterested teen. They had two members left too. All eyes were on the last four people to scale the wall. The crowd cheered wildly.

Lydia put her butt up against the wall and hunched over, with her hands on her knees. What madness was this? Was Dad going to stand on *her*?

"Lydia!" I screamed. "What are you thinking?"

She threw me a look and shouted, "I'm tougher than I look!"

"Mom, get up." I shook her. "We've got to help Dad. But my arms are beat from lifting you."

Mom scrambled to brace herself and lean over the wall. I shook out my arms. My hands and arms were so tired, I could barely make a fist with my right hand. I wasn't sure I could be of any help.

My mind started whirring. Instead of leaning over and relying on my arms, I had a better idea. I straddled the wall, dropping my left leg over the side so Dad could grab on to it. My legs still had some strength left in them. I wasn't sure he could reach me, but it was the best I could do.

Dad managed to climb on top of Lydia's knees and then, onto her back. I could see Lydia's legs shaking. She wouldn't last long. Dad faced the wall and found his balance. He stood. Then he bent his knees and jumped.

He grabbed my foot as Lydia tumbled to the ground. While Dad hung in the air, his grip around my foot was slipping.

"Grab my hand, you big jerk," Mom yelled.

Mom extended herself over the wall as far as she could. The top of it must have been cutting into her hip-bones, but she didn't complain. "Georgia, sit on my feet!" she ordered.

Georgia did as she was told.

I wasn't sure how Dad, with his recent bad fall, was managing. He willed himself to lunge for Mom's hand. Lydia had scrambled back to her feet and was supporting one of Dad's feet with both her arms raised as high above her head as she could stretch.

"Hurry!" Lydia screamed.

I didn't know she had all *this* in her.

Dad wrapped his arm around my leg and I gritted my teeth. Mom pulled so hard on his other arm I thought she might pop his shoulder out of its socket. But the old dude made it. I wasn't sure how it happened because, by the end, I was starting to see stars. I tumbled over to the platform, grateful to no longer have the edge of the wall between my legs.

Flat on his back, Dad gasped for air.

Mom was sitting next to him, struggling to catch her breath too. Suddenly, she slapped his stomach. Then the two of them started laughing.

"It's not done yet!" I reminded them. I looked down at Lydia. It was just her and one lone teenage boy left. It would come down to this.

Lydia glanced over at her competitor before looking up at me. "Anybody going to help me?" she yelled.

"How? What do you want me to do?" I hollered back.

"Just catch me!" she bellowed.

I poked my parents. "Get up!"

The three of us leaned over and waited for Lydia.

"Just use your good side," I reminded Dad. "Lean down as far as you can."

Lydia backed up. She backed up farther than I thought she should. The teenage boy was already hanging, holding on to one of his teammates, who were also leaning over the wall.

Then Lydia ran. It was a power run. I'd seen this run before. It was the run of the unbeatable robot in *Terminator 3*. But it was also the run she used when vaulting. Her arms pumped powerfully, and even as she approached the wall, Lydia did not slow down.

I watched with a mixture of absolute delight and shock as my sister ran *up* the wall several steps before lunging for Dad's hand.

Who is this person? I wondered.

Dad's good arm was all he needed. He lifted Lydia over the wall.

For a second, Team Park did not move. We stared at each other, basking in the moment. We had all made it over the *Wall of Doom*.

"The finish line!" Georgia said. She headed to the stairs with a raised fist. "Park Power!"

Team Park assembled chaotically and ran — together.

28

A HEART OF GRIT

THE FIELD BETWEEN THE BOTTOM OF THE STAIRS and the orange flags signaling the end of the course looked like a combat zone. There were a few abandoned shoes, several of the adhesive stickers participants were supposed to wear, and, strangely, a pair of mud-soaked shorts.

Team Park ran together, with Georgia trailing slightly behind. I made sure to stay with her as best as I could. Lydia crossed the line first, as she apparently had superpowers that she'd long hidden. Followed by Mom and Dad and, bringing up the rear, me and Georgia.

The final team had gotten the teenager over the wall and was fast approaching, but they couldn't catch Team Park.

In a messy heap, Team Park laid down on the ground. Everybody tried to catch their breath.

Georgia said, "That was fun."

"It sure was." My chest heaved. I had never agreed with Georgia more.

Darren ran up, slid on his knees, and embraced me while I was still lying on the ground.

"Dude, you were *amazing*!" Darren beamed. His jacket was now covered in mud.

"We're second to last!" I told him.

He was startled by my response. "So? You had a broken wrist a few months ago. And your team had a three-year-old."

"Three and a half!" Georgia informed Darren.

"Three and a half." Darren smiled at her before turning back to me. "You did amazing. Your team did amazing." Darren held out his fist for each of us to tap.

"Really?"

"Really."

I was last and he waited for me to sit up. "Thanks." My knuckles tapped lightly against his. "In a way, we're here because of you."

Darren looked taken aback. "What do you mean?"

"You told me how much fun ninja training was. I was kind of inspired."

It was the first time I had ever seen Darren look a little self-conscious.

"Originally, I was ninja training. But I couldn't do the Dominator Ninja thing in Seattle like I really wanted to because I tweaked my wrist again. So, we ended up here instead."

"Ah." He nodded. "You know, you're not here because of *me*. You're here because of *you*. I may have introduced you to the Dominator lifestyle, but if you don't have it in you, you don't do it."

"It's not quite the same as this," I said, pointing to the Soiled Pants racecourse.

"This has the same heart. Just messier events."

"Dirty ninja!" Georgia said loudly.

"Exactly. Just a really dirty ninja." Darren smiled.

We all fell silent for a second.

"I gotta go help do some end-of-event housekeeping." Darren glanced over his shoulder at the other staff members setting up tables. "I would love to see you at a ninja event soon." He winked.

Then, at the exact same moment, he and I both said, "There's always next year."

We laughed and then waved goodbye, and I was happy to just sit and relax for a while.

Now that we were done, and I had time to breathe, reality finally hit me. We had finished, and that was something, but there wasn't going to be a medal for me or Team Park. I was too exhausted to feel anything but numb.

A voice over the loudspeaker said, "All participants who finished, please assemble in five minutes for the medal ceremony."

I hadn't realized that there must have been teams that dropped out *during* the race. It had been too chaotic to really notice everything.

I watched the organizers set up a podium, just like at the Olympics, for the medal winners. One center piece, higher than the other two levels surrounding it.

As expected, Team Gouda was first. They didn't even look tired. Their real name was Team Vankemper, but to me, they would always be Team Gouda. We all clapped as they received their gold medals around their necks. Team We ♥ Corgis won the silver, and Team Good Looks & Books took the bronze. My lips were pursed until all top three teams got their medals.

After the ceremony, I was really ready to head home. But the man with the microphone kept talking. "For those who are veterans of the Soiled Pants races, you all know how tough these races are."

Somebody screamed, "Darn right!" The rest of the crowd chuckled.

"So, because you know how much work, how much grit it takes to get it done, I would like to give a special award to our two new families who worked hard to finish their first-ever Soiled Pants: Family Edition! Give it up for Team Park and Team Hobbs Roofing & Solar Panels!"

My mind went blank. My body went into stasis. *Special award*.

People started to clap and pat us on the back. My eyes darted from my parents to Lydia and then down to Georgia.

Lydia pulled at my arm. "Come on. They're calling us."

Mom picked up Georgia. Dad gestured to the podium area with his head. "Ev, let's go." He smiled broadly and, despite his aching shoulder, there was a spring in his step.

We made our way to the front and found spots next to the MC. Team Park on his right side, Team Hobbs Roofing & Solar Panels on his left.

I clasped my hands in front of me and stared out at the crowd of dirty Soiled Pants racers who clapped for us. What a sight. Everybody was filthy, but that wasn't the most obvious thing. The most obvious thing about them was that they all looked *happy*.

"Team Park! Team Hobbs Roofing & Solar Panels!" the MC said. "This was your very first race! You finished seventh and eighth respectively." A small round of applause followed.

Seventh! That was higher than I realized.

In the bleachers, Aaron and Davey waved their flag

again. Luckily, Aaron had put his shirt back on. When the applause died down, they screamed, "Team Park!"

The MC continued, "In addition, we introduced some new challenges this year. So, I must commend you! What an accomplishment. It is extremely difficult to finish one of these courses on your first try."

"Tell me about it!" somebody from the audience yelled.

The rest of the crowd laughed.

"So, to welcome you to the Soiled Pants family, we present to you a completion trophy!"

Another staff member came forward holding a small tray with two trophies.

The MC picked up the trophy and was going to hand it to Dad, but Dad refused it and told him to hand it to me instead. The trophies were about as tall as my hand. It wasn't a human figure or a cup, like you'd expect. Instead, it was a design that looked a lot like the medals they had just given out — a pair of shorts sticking out from a mud puddle. I mean, there couldn't have possibly been a cooler trophy than this one.

I received the trophy, gave a little bow of thanks, and held it up with one hand.

"Team Park! Team Park!" It was Darren. He continued to chant until a few other people, led by Aaron and Davey, caught on and started to chant with him.

When the MC turned to the other team, the chanting for our team faded away, but nobody started it up again for Team Hobbs Roofing & Solar Panels. Their name doesn't roll off the tongue easily.

When we went back to join the crowd of competitors, I stared at the trophy in my hand.

⇒ COMPLETED ⇐
SOILED PANTS
FAMILY EDITION

"And now, before we let you all go clean yourselves up, our special draw! For those eight teams who completed today's event, Agile Ninja Training Centre has generously donated a chance to win one of their now sold-out gym memberships!"

Sold out? My heart dropped. We wouldn't be able to buy memberships even if we could have afforded it.

A staff member with a glass bowl filled with slips of paper appeared. *You never win stuff like this,* I reminded myself.

When the MC put down the microphone, I was elbowed. Darren was standing right next to me. "How you feeling *now*?" he asked.

I swallowed the hard lump that had been sitting in my throat.

"Okay." There wasn't time to tell him that my stomach was a mess and that things were happening so fast I wasn't really able to think straight.

Darren leaned over and said, "I just want to tell you . . ."

But before I knew it the MC was sticking his hand in the bowl, and I couldn't focus on what Darren was saying. Why was he talking to me *now*? Couldn't he see that something important was happening?

The MC had selected his piece of paper. He was prolonging my agony by making a real show of it. He opened the paper ever so slowly. I just wanted to run up there and rip it out of his hands! While he read the paper, he made an exaggerated face of shock and surprise.

"Hurry up and tell us!" Georgia yelled.

The crowd roared with laughter.

"Congratulations, Team Sidhu's Plumbing!" The MC held the piece of paper out to show the audience.

I felt my spine collapse. We hadn't won. I looked up to the sky and tried to keep it together.

"It's okay," Lydia said, rubbing my back. "I think Dad will build you more stuff in the backyard. You can still train."

"Why?" Darren asked.

"He wants to do more ninja training," Lydia told him.

"Perfect!" Darren said.

For the first time, I was genuinely annoyed with Darren. "What are you talking about?"

He looked puzzled. "Didn't you hear me?"

"No! I was trying to listen to the MC!"

"My bad. My timing wasn't so great."

I sighed. "I don't get anything you're saying right now."

The MC said, "Thank you all for coming and participating today! We hope you had a blast! We hope to see you next time! Let's keep soiling our pants!"

The crowd cheered wildly for a while and then, when the laughter and the clapping slowed down, people started to disperse.

"Come on," Mom said to us. "Let's clean up."

"I'll just keep Evan for one more minute," Darren told her.

My family started to walk away while I stayed with Darren.

He glanced around and waited for the talking around us to fade away before he said, quietly, "I'll be starting work at Agile Ninja Training Centre when it opens. I'll be a part-time coach and their part-time in-house rehab. That's what I was trying to tell you before."

"You will?" My eyes were wide open. "That *was* you on their promotional video!"

"Yeah, it was!" He did a big belly laugh. "When you finished at Kids Only Physio, I kind of knew I wasn't going to be there much longer, but my work contract at Agile Ninja wasn't all settled yet, so I couldn't really say anything."

"You get to do ninja training as your *job*? It's like a dream come true for you, isn't it?"

He smiled. "Yup. I'm lucky."

As soon as he said "lucky," I thought about Davey's nickname for me. Turns out Lucky Break wasn't so lucky. There was no free gym membership for me.

I wished I could see Darren at the gym. He'd make a really great coach. And if I ever hurt my wrist again, he'd be right there!

"There are lots of perks with working at the gym," Darren continued.

"Ev, I think it's time to wash up." Dad had come back to collect me. He pointed to the hose station.

"Okay, I'll be right there." It looked like the water hoses were the only thing that had turned out the way I'd expected. "I gotta go," I said to Darren. The mud was starting to dry and felt tight on my skin. "It was nice seeing you again."

"You can keep seeing me!" Darren said.

Unsure what he meant, I scrunched my eyebrows. "At physio?"

"As I was saying, one of the perks of working at Agile Ninja is . . ." He left his words hanging.

I leaned in. "Is what?"

"Guest passes."

"Guest passes?" I asked.

"For guests."

"For guests?"

"For you."

"For *me*?"

He reached into his pocket and pulled out a plastic bag. Inside was a small booklet of tickets, stapled together.

I couldn't pick my jaw up off the ground.

"I'll see you there." Before he turned to leave, he tapped the top of the trophy I was still holding and winked.

I placed the trophy and the bag of tickets in a safe spot near one of the staff tents and ran to the hoses. Darren was pretty smart to put the tickets in the bag before he gave them to me.

The water was *freezing* but that's what made it fun. There was no better way to end the day than to wash the mud off our faces.

I flicked a stream of water gently at Georgia, who shrieked every time the water hit her. With her, I was mild. I saved being annoying for Lydia. She was tough — she could handle it.

She could dish it out as well as she could receive it, and we ended up having an epic battle of the hoses.

By the end, there wasn't a single speck of mud left on us.

Even Mom and Dad seemed to enjoy the hose station. Mom seemed giddy whenever she pointed the hose in Dad's direction. For a tough guy, Dad squirmed and wiggled and yelped endlessly at the touch of water from a garden hose.

When we were about ready to leave, Dad said, "I think you will all agree that my experience with rugby finally came in handy."

We all groaned loudly, and I aimed my hose in his direction. Lydia followed with a hose of her own. Just when he thought he was all clean, Mom threw some mud at him. Georgia managed to throw somebody's abandoned shoe in Dad's direction too.

All of the day's frustrations and hardships were forgotten after all the laughter.

Before we were ready to leave for real, I had to do it. Just once while we were here. I held the hose straight up in the air, pressed my thumb over the end of it to add pressure and change the flow of the water, and then held it as high over my head as I could. There it was. My wet confetti, raining down on me.

29

A LUCKY BREAK

AFTER THE HOSE STATION WE GOT FREE SOUVENIR towels. I rubbed the towel all over my hair and draped it over my shoulders as we left the event area. My first trip to a Soiled Pants race hadn't worked out exactly as I had hoped, but the end result was still pretty decent. Summer officially ended tomorrow, and my Summer of Fun goals had been unlocked.

We stopped by the taco truck in the parking lot for a late lunch and picked a sunny spot in Bear Creek Park to eat and relax.

Aaron and Davey passed us while we waited for our food. Aaron's dad honked his horn loudly at us and yelled out the window. "Awesome job, Team Park!"

We waved back, and Aaron and Davey stuck their heads out the window and waved frantically.

"See you at school Tuesday!" Aaron yelled.

"That was fun!" Davey said. Then they drove away.

When our order was ready, we all sat down to the serious task of eating. Everybody was *hungry*.

Sitting crossed-legged on the grass, I placed the trophy in between my legs as I inhaled four tacos. With a full stomach, I lay down on the towel and let the sun warm me.

Dad started on his second burrito and said, "So, I guess you're not going back to your soccer team?"

I burst out laughing. "Not a chance." I sat up. "You know what? *This* is the only team sport for me."

"Yeah!" Mom said. "While it seems like an individual event, we had to work as a team to . . ."

"Not eat more mud than necessary!" I joked. I was glad the carnitas had finally overpowered the taste of the mud in my mouth.

Dad chewed his burrito. "Huh. I never thought about Soiled Pants like a true team sport."

"That's what happens when you're stuck viewing the world through a traditional lens. You pigeonhole people and ideas," Lydia said. "Even yourself. You miss out on stuff."

Fun stuff, I thought. I looked fondly at my sister. When she ran for class president and then, when she was old enough, prime minister, she would have my vote every time.

"Lydia." Dad cleared his throat.

She looked in his direction.

"You were pretty amazing," he said. "That run you did . . ."

"It's nothing special. Just my normal run for the vault." She shrugged. "Gymnastics isn't all ribbons and hairbows. You should make time to come see me at practice more often."

"You've got Park Power," Dad said. "More than I realized."

Lydia smiled shyly and ate a tortilla chip.

"Was I a good dirty ninja teammate?" Georgia asked me. She picked the meat out of her taco.

"The best three-and-a-half dirty ninja teammate that ever lived."

"I like Ehbun." She stood to give me a hug. "But I don't like blue porta-potty, so I won't use it. Even though I have to pee." She pointed to the line of them set up outside the event. I was glad she didn't ask me to cram myself in there next to her. That would have been a real low point in an otherwise pretty good day.

Mom leaned over. "I thought ahead. She's got swim pull-ups on. Waterproof." She tapped her head to remind me how smart moms could be. They really do think about everything.

We all fell silent, and I let my food digest. I realized that I hadn't even mentioned the guest passes yet! Now seemed like the perfect time.

"Darren gave me something pretty cool at the end," I said.

"Oh yeah?" Lydia seemed interested. She wiped salt off her fingertips.

I fished the tickets out of my still-damp shorts. "Guest passes to Agile Ninja Training Centre."

"Wow! That was nice of him!" Mom said. She reached out to take a look at the contents of the plastic bag.

"He's going to start work there."

"No more Kids Only Physio?" she asked.

I shook my head.

"Will you take me when it opens?" I asked Mom.

"Of course!"

"'Cause I've got to get ready for Dominator Ninja next year."

Dad cleared his throat again. "Maybe I could . . . come with you? You know. Try it out."

I felt kind of glow-y inside. "Sure, Dad. I'd like that." I stuck the tickets back into my pocket.

"Ehbun is the Dirty Ninja!" Georgia exclaimed.

Lydia said, "We can get new T-shirts!"

"Well, if the name fits . . ." I laughed. It seems I'd finally have to accept it. Just call me the Dirty Ninja. "Get a mucky-brown-colored T-shirt, please."

On the car ride home, we were very quiet. The euphoric high of the day was wearing thin and everybody was realizing how tired they were.

I held the trophy in my hands. It was hard to let go of it. But when we got home, I knew exactly where it was going to go.

Out of the corner of my eye, I caught Lydia staring at me. I met her gaze and she smiled before playfully punching me in the shoulder.

"I didn't know you were Spider-Man," I said to her. In my mind, I played back the image of her doing a power sprint toward the wall.

"Spider-*Girl* or Spider-*Woman*, please," she said. "No, actually it should be Spider-*Person*, just to be inclusive." She blew a small bubble of gum and popped it immediately.

"Seriously, did you attach suction cups to your shoes?" I asked.

"They installed a warped wall at my gymnastics gym a few weeks ago," she admitted. "This wall didn't have a curve, so I couldn't go up as far as I can normally."

My mouth dropped. "You never said anything about a warped wall!"

"Didn't I?" She looked surprised.

"That's poor communication," Georgia said. "Second-best book says so."

I turned to stare at Georgia, who was gazing out the window.

"What exactly is your second-best book called anyway?" I asked.

Georgia reached into the hanging pocket attached to the right side of her car seat. It appeared that she was just about to remove something, but instead, she froze. "This is my secret spot. Don't look."

"Seriously?" I asked.

"Always serious," Georgia replied. "Just like Daddy."

Lydia and I made a show of looking away, even though we were seated right next to her.

"Okay, I'm ready." Georgia held a small board book in her hands. It was a copy of *Goodnight Moon*. "It's called *Let's Talk*."

Puzzled, I looked over at Lydia, who looked equally confused, but we kept quiet.

Georgia flipped to the first page. She cleared her throat. "First, try your best. Even if it's hard."

Mom turned in her front seat to listen.

Georgia flipped to the next page.

"People should talk nicely to family, not bossy and rude," Georgia said, staring at the page. "Shouting voices is sometimes scary."

Mom's face flushed. Dad kept his eyes straight ahead at first, but then stole a glance at Georgia through the rearview mirror.

"If it don't hurt a little, you ain't doing it right!" Georgia said, flipping to the next page.

"Team Park finished dirty ninja race all together. The end." Georgia slammed the book closed.

"Is this art imitating life?" Lydia asked herself, confused.

"That's a good book," I told Georgia. "Why is it only your second-best book?"

"Not as funny as hedgehog-and-unicorn book."

"Some good lessons in that second-best book, huh?" Lydia stared at our parents.

Dad held out his hand over the middle console. "Some good reminders, that's for sure."

Mom clasped her hand over his and glanced at him. She then turned to look out the window, but she didn't let go of his hand.

"What do you want to do tomorrow?" Mom asked.

Everybody laughed.

"Come back here to cheer for Darren, obviously," I said.

Nobody objected to the idea. I was going to sit in the stands and cheer loudly for my excellent physiotherapist.

"You know, the Dominator Ninja event in Seattle is in a few weeks. We should go cheer for Darren there too,"

I suggested. "I'd love to see him reach the top of Pinnacle Peak and press the button for the confetti bomb."

"We could stop for some popcorn shrimp from Ivar's on the way there," Dad said. "It could be fun."

"It *will* be fun," I said.

I wanted to see Darren achieve his dream at Dominator Ninja because he had seen me achieve mine — finally, after a couple of lucky breaks, I had found my thing.

ACKNOWLEDGMENTS

I have this row of towering western red cedars at the very back of my property. They are actually not "mine" — they are situated in a right-of-way and technically belong to the City of Vancouver. But the city never comes by to take care of them, so for all intents and purposes, the trees are mine.

I will say that I love trees. I will also say that I don't love these trees on my property. I am blessed (or cursed) with *messy* trees. Are you familiar with the term "flagging"? When referring to trees (cedars in particular), it means that the trees, although evergreen, shed foliage each year. Ridiculous amounts of orange foliage.

Because I'm outside (a lot) cleaning up tree droppings, I have a considerable amount of time to think. Aside from the obvious *I hate these trees,* I also think things like: *What can I do with this useless space crowded with trees that is "mine" but not really mine?* Then, I rake and shove debris into the compost bin. But one day, I had a different thought: *Wouldn't it be a good idea to hang stuff from these trees so the kids could play back here?* That's how *Team Park* was born.

The book has kids doing fun things in their backyard, but in reality, I never did make a playground for my own kids; they are teenagers now and don't "play," so I don't think they are too mad at me about it. They are mad at me about lots of other things instead. I adore them anyway.

After the book was done, the racoons got me back and started using the space between the trees as a latrine. Funny enough, I'd mentioned this situation in *Peter Lee's Notes from the Field* — not actually expecting it to happen in my own yard. In the end, the only thing I ever actually attached to the trees was chicken wire to discourage those little bandits from getting too comfy. I think they finally moved on.

I did get an idea that resulted in a published book because of those trees, so while I still do despise their presence, I have come to peace with their existence.

While I'm blabbing, I should also note that I don't know a thing about rugby. It's only used in my book because I just happened to be standing next to a brightly lit playing field one autumn night while a practice was going on. I was waiting for my daughter to finish a school event. Without anything else to do, I watched the rugby team. Over and over again, they practiced tossing one player straight up into the air. *What on earth are they doing?* I wondered, watching with complete fascination. I went home and did some research. The lineout. Somehow, I managed to make this one play in rugby an important part of the ending of this story, which, at the time, I wasn't sure how to finish. Isn't life wonderfully unpredictable?

I'm going to thank the usual people I always thank. I never take this journey that starts with a wild idea to a finished book for granted, and my fabulous editor, Lynne Missen, and my wonderful agent, Laurel Symonds, are always by my side. The whole team at Tundra too! From the art department to the sales and marketing teams, you have all been marvelous to work with over so many books.

Many thanks to Misa Sugiura for her very excellent advice. I also shouldn't forget to thank Laura for reading an early draft.

Finally, Chris Choi, thank you for the cover art, which could not be more perfect!